MW01485702

The Real World

Monitor

We Print News Other Papers Dare Not

A Novel By
Brad Glenn

OFF
THE
BOOKS

For Sarah and her unending support and unconditional love, and the other love of my life, Ella

Special Thanks to Lisa Ward Mather and to the Inkhorn Society Members: Darcy Rust, Samantha Mick, Kelly Chen, Matt Simmonds, Sue Hoffman, Bradley Pearce, and Elizabeth Vail.

1

The red Miata, clean and sparkling, top down in the summer heat, cut through the last of the L.A. smog as it sped down the highway. The tall buildings of civilization were already growing pale and small, the houses becoming further and further apart, and the last of the big box outlet stores finally gave way to open plains, rocks, peaks, and valleys.

"We're going to die out here," Brooke said over the yipping of the Pomeranian in the back seat. Her pink Bobbi Brown painted fingernails digging deep into the seat belt as the wind whipped her long blond hair around.

"We're not going to die," Nate sighed. Nate Crossfield hadn't shaved in a few days, what with having to move, leave his office, and, of course, the scandal. Normally he wore a dress shirt, leaving the top two buttons undone, and a tweed suit jacket. He felt it gave him the proper air of a reporter. He always wanted to look the part. Today, v-neck t-shirt and jeans.

The Pomeranian, Toodles, continued to yip from her crate. She had been confined to her crate since the trip started. Maybe in the city, top up, she was fine in the back seat, short trips to the vet, carried around stores in Brooke's purse, but, since leaving L.A., she wouldn't calm down. While still free roaming at the start of the trip, after Brooke and Nate had sombrely locked the deadbolt of their apartment for the last time, dropped the keys off with the concierge, and unceremoniously and discreetly left the city, Brooke had worried she'd make a leap for it, bail out of the car and race back to the comfort of the city. They had rummaged through the small trunk, stuffed full of everything they'd need until the movers arrived. Luckily, they had the foresight to pack the crate instead of allowing the movers to toss it in the back of their truck with the rest of Nate and Brooke's nearly fifteen years of acquisitions. They'd locked the dog in, and although usually she'd calmed when put into her den-like little enclosure, on this trip it had merely agitated her more.

"I don't know why we're going to this hellhole anyway," Brooke said, her lips pursed tightly until they were almost as purple as her dress. Her eyes never left the road, yet Nate felt scrutinized, as if they were burrowing into his skull.

The desert reached out far in front of them. The drive was a boring one. Few turns, few rest areas, no stops of interest. Even the landscape, which ranged from small brush to the rocky desert, with a few gnarled yucca trees but otherwise devoid of landmarks, added to the emptiness around them. There was nothing but the brownish red desert ground, occasional creosote bush, and the blue cloudless sky. There was also that single black stripe of highway ahead of them. The traffic had all been left behind as commuters from L.A. turned off until the road was empty. Nate felt an eeriness to the desert, something he hadn't felt in years, something that someone might not suspect if they hadn't lived in one long enough. He remembered how the isolation gets to a person, as does the otherworldliness of the terrain.

"I grew up here. It's really not that bad," he mumbled under his breath. Trying to explain himself wouldn't help now. Her life was turned upside down, and she wasn't to blame. He couldn't even defend himself. He could just sit there and take it. Seven hours of road ahead of him, deep into the desert, and all he could do was take it. "Not like we had much choice anyway."

"And whose fault is that?"

More yipping from the back seat. Toodles always barked when they fought. Then again, Toodles barked when they laughed, when they cooked, cleaned, made love. Toodles just barked at nothing sometimes.

"Mine!" Nate steamed. This wasn't about clarification. This wasn't about clearing the air or hearing her feelings. This was about shaming. This was making sure Nate felt like an absolute piece of shit. It was just too bad he deserved it. "It was my fault! I know! I fucked everything up, and I put us here!"

Nate put his hand up to his mouth, as if keeping his thoughts from escaping. He rubbed his stubble and rested his fingers on the scar across his left cheek. It ran from the outer corner of his eye down to his jaw, still pink and puffy after all these years, and he often found himself running his fingers over it when stuck in stressful situations. Like when he'd been caught.

He'd gotten the scar when he was eight years old. It was a hot summer day, and Nate wasn't the type to hang out with a large group of friends, so he found himself spending his mornings at the small library in Red Valley. Then, book in hand, he'd walk home through the streets, reading as he walked. He could navigate the streets easily, had memorized every turn, every wooden curb, every rock in the dirt roads. Of course, the day they paved the streets everything changed slightly and he didn't notice the paving crew. He walked past the sawhorses and construction signs, and tripped onto some rebar. He cut himself up, got a face full of stitches and scared the hell out of his mother. His father was unconcerned. He had a boys-will-be-boys attitude to everything and his busy work schedule with the military gave him a distance that bordered on neglect. Nate would've preferred neglect, though, instead of his father's harshness, his bitterness, his violence. The strange thing was that

Nate's father, Werner, had nearly the same scar down his face. He got his while hunting in the forests up North. Still, same scar, father and son.

"Yeah, and now suddenly it's my problem. Mine!" Brooke spoke with a spite that cut Nate up, sliced him and stabbed him right through. He set his teeth on edge, jaw clenched, but Brooke wasn't letting up. "Now I'm stuck in some shit town in the middle of nowhere! You said you'd take care of me! You promised! You told me you'd treat me like a princess!"
The wind blew through the convertible, and while it was cooling under the sweltering heat of a desert sun, the constant rumble of the wind in his ears, his light brown hair, normally fixed in place through ample hair products, flipped and swatted his face, making it yet another source of irritation. The Pomeranian, hers, of course, picked up from the same breeder that all the wives of the big name journalists used, yipped and yapped constantly. Nate normally would've turned and yelled at it to shut up, or better yet, have left it in their apartment for the next tenants who might want a dog with an impressive pedigree in order to fit in with the elite crowd, but he knew better. Brooke saw the dog as her last connection to high society, so for all his anger towards her, all his rage and hurt and shame, he had to sympathize.

"You know why this happened," Nate pleaded, clenching the steering wheel. For all the patience he was attempting to muster, he was still exploding inside. "No one would hire me! My career is a wreck, and you're just... Look. The only reason the Monitor hired me is because of my Dad's good name in town? Right? That's my Dad trying to help us!" The words sounded ingenuine coming out of his mouth.

His father's good name was a bit of a joke. He wasn't a warm man, wasn't particularly kind to the rest of the townsfolk, and wasn't exactly personable. But he was a soldier. When the fire broke out in Merle Winslow's house, Werner Crossfield was there before the volunteer firefighters, pulling Merle and his wife out of the smoky interior, even running back in for their ragged sixteen-year-old cat. He'd achieved hero status in Red Valley over that one, but Nate couldn't figure out why he was in town at three in the morning when he was supposed to be on base.

"Hah!" Brooke laughed sarcastically. "Some help. What'd he do, call from the hospital? Rant about the pudding?"

"Fuck... just... just let it go!"

"Yeah, I'll let it go. You fuck up at your job, now we're overdrawn at the bank and leaving all my friends to go to some buttfuck town, but yeah, I'll just let that go. That's totally fair."

"You could've gotten a job! I mean, why was it always on me? You used to work!"

"I can't work. I have a disability."

"Alopecia isn't a disability!"

"It's anxiety!"

2

Red Valley isn't your typical desert town, not that any desert town is exactly typical. There's something about it that attracts the strange. It permeates everything about the town, and while the townsfolk attempt to remain oblivious, everyone feels it. No one speaks of it. They live their lives, work their jobs, attend church on Sunday.

Edgar Catafalque saw things differently. Edgar Catafalque: Obscurologist. That was on all of his business cards, not that he handed them out all that often. Edgar was the kind of guy who'd have lined his hat in tinfoil if he'd thought that would work. It wouldn't, and Edgar had the insight and experience to know that. He wore a tan trench coat in the middle of summer, white shirt and black half windsor. He checked over his shoulder for the fifth time as he pulled into the lot in his 1967 Buick Wildcat, also known as his house, and tossed his cigarette butt out of the window. Then, like a ripple in a velvet sack, slinked into the clinic that had popped up on the edge of town. It was better than heading down to Mexico. Well, faster, anyway. The door chimed as he entered the air-conditioned coolness of the waiting room.

It was nothing to look at. A few old cushioned benches to sit on, left over from when Dr. Perkins retired and closed his dental clinic, and a chipped counter. The whole building felt more like a pawn shop than a plastic surgery clinic.

"Mr. Catafalque?" Dr. Tarentola called from the back in a thick Eastern European accent. Edgar looked down at the stained linoleum tiles on the floor, cobwebbed corners. He suspected there'd still be time to sneak out, but no, it was too dire. Too many people had seen his face. Too many people wanted the knowledge he had accumulated over years of searching through occult tomes and cryptozoological hot spots.

"Yup," he called back determinedly, "even on time."

"Beautiful!" Dr. Tarentola said, coming out from the back. He was a small man, thick, moist lips contrasted by his small eyes and bald head. He reached out a clammy hand to shake Edgar's. "We're all ready, follow me," he said, holding Edgar's hand uncomfortably to guide him towards the back.

"Thanks for doing this so quickly," Edgar said, unsure of how much he should actually divulge. "I have to change this face. I need to look different. You can probably fill in the blanks."

"I get a lot of face alterations here. On the run from the police, possibly? No, don't answer that. It's really none of my business," he said, directing Edgar to the dilapidated dental chair. "Hang up your coat, roll up your sleeves, and put this on." He handed Edgar a long paper bib with a metal clasp along the back. His attempt at a smile was more disturbing than comforting, yellow teeth with wide and irregular spacing, as he patted the seat of the chair with hand. The inside of the operating room wasn't much cleaner than the rest of the office. At least the surgical equipment lining the counters looked sparkling and clean under the fluorescent lighting. "Now, before we start, you need to sign a few forms, and, of course, secure payment."

Edgar wasn't unaccustomed to being in compromising situations. Sure, flat on his back with a strange plastic surgeon wasn't the most comfortable position to be in, but Edgar had been in worse. He was, when a young man, quite average. That all changed when he'd stumbled upon a small bookstore, deep in the dark corners of his own backwards home town. The Mystagogue, run by an armless conspiracist with a penchant for drama. "I'll not sell you the book you want," the man had said, "only the book you need." Edgar had directed to pick up the Liber Secretorium. It had taught him the mystic greetings of the Cynocephali, the pathways of the secret labyrinth deep beneath the Vatican, Planet X and hundreds of other secrets. It plunged him deep into the world of occult investigations, psychic overdosing and procuring information from many of the world's most deadly organizations, like the Odd Fellows, The Thirteen Clandestine Levels of the Veiled Priors, or even the Scientology Apostles.

"I have the cash right here," Edgar said, pulling out seven one-hundred dollar bills, "and… if there's any way we can keep this off of the books…" Edgar added another three hundred dollars to the handful of bills.

"Of course," Dr. Tarentola said, pulling those large lips back into his wide, unsettling smile. He stuffed the bills into the pocket of his white laboratory jacket and lowered the back of the chair until Edgar was on his back. "The surgery is a very simple one, and very few risks, although there are risks implicit with anaesthesia." Dr. Tarentola strapped Edgar's wrist to the arm of the dental chair with a coarse tan-coloured strap and scratched metal buckle. Then he calmly and quietly walked around Edgar, looking down at the prone man, and strapped the other arm in place as well. He then swabbed Edgar's arm with a cotton ball soaked in rubbing alcohol. "Just relax. Small pinch coming up. Like a mosquito bite."

"So you do this alone?" Edgar asked. He hadn't really expected much for a seven hundred dollar plastic surgery job, but it did seem odd that the man wouldn't have an assistant of some kind. "I guess you get what you pay for."

"My assistants are washing up as we speak. This isn't brain surgery we're doing here. It's a face lift and a few implants to alter your appearance. Very routine. Don't concern yourself with the small details of the operation. Just close your eyes and when you wake up, your life will be completely different."

No cars in the parking lot, save the Wildcat and a rusted Impala. Silence in the building. Dr. Tarentola was lying, and Edgar became suddenly acutely aware of it. He railed against the straps holding him down, yanking violently from side to side. He rocked forward, biting at the heavy leather straps on his arms, but it wasn't enough to overcome their restraint. Dr. Tarentola easily shoved him back in the dental chair and pierced the soft skin on the bend of Edgar's elbow with the hypodermic needle.

"Bastard!" Edgar yelled, still struggling to get the plastic surgeon off of him. The man smelled like sweat, breath like fermented fish. "Who are you working for?" Then, for a moment there was a taste in his mouth, not unlike garlic tinged with copper, as the anaesthetic took effect. Then, nothing.

Dr. Tarentola's knife sliced a slow, deliberate half circle from Edgar's temples to his hairline and down again. The knife was nearly silent as it rounded outside of his ears and down his jawline just below the chin. The blood oozed out, soaking into Edgar's slicked back black hair, staining the collar of his shirt, dripping down the headrest of the dental chair and pooling on the floor. Dr. Tarentola continued cutting sinuous chunks of flesh, scraping the skull, pulling and yanking, violently at times, separating skin from bone.

Outside one wouldn't know what was going on. In fact, the only car to pass by was a red Miata just entering town, the woman inside complaining "what a shit-hole," as it passed. The driver exhausted after hours of straight roads and constant complaints.

Outside, one wouldn't suspect a doctor with a black leather briefcase, possibly even a doctor wearing a blood-stained laboratory coat as Dr. Tarentola was, would be up to anything untoward as he walked to his Impala, and pulled out of the packed dirt parking lot and away into the desert.

Outside, one couldn't even hear Edgar's screams as he woke up.

3

Built in 1937, the house was two stories, faded wooden shutters over the pale blue wooden siding. Shingles sun-baked and curled, warped windows from an earlier time. Two steps up on a rickety set of stairs to the entrance and an old door that'd been there since before Nate was born, scratched and splintered from the decades of use.

The house had settled over the years as well. What was once a perfectly plumb door frame was now angled, so much so that some of the doors needed to be shoved to open, while others closed by themselves. After all these years of sitting, empty, in the dry heat of the desert, there wasn't a right angle in the place.

It was a crooked house. It was Nate's house.

Nate's father, Werner, bought the house before Nate was born. It wasn't always run down, two stories of peeling paint and rusted hinges. Nate's mother had kept the rock garden immaculate, desert trees pruned and cared for, for as long as she was there. They kept the hitching rail, as a part of history although a horse had never been hitched to it for as long as Nate knew of it. Sadly, as his father's health declined so did the house. The desert isn't kind to man-made structures. Nate's father hadn't lived in the house for five years. Not since the stroke.

The red Miata pulling up the block, passing by the houses of the neighbours, all strangely close to each other even with vast expanse of the desert just beyond, seemed out of place. It was too shiny, too modern, in this place of dust and history.

It pulled into the driveway, and Stan, caught off guard not only by the foreign nature of a new car in this old town, and the fact no one had pulled into the driveway since the ambulance took Werner away, stopped tilling the soil of his dry garden with his hoe and leaned on it. Stan lived next door and seemed the sort of man who would enjoy the harsh conditions and intense heat of living in a desert. Sweat dripped down his shirtless chest, seeping into his overalls, as Stan leaned against the old barnwood fence separating their properties as he watched the car roll to a stop behind Werner's old brown pickup shrouded in the webs of funnel spiders. The crooked house had been empty for so long it seemed like an invasion for anyone to go into it, even into the driveway.

"Oh God," Brooke said as the car pulled to a halt, "don't tell me it has come to this."

"It's not that bad, Brooke," Nate said, feeble smile on his face, "I grew up in this house. It's a bit run down, but we can do something with this place. We can spruce it up, give it a paint job..."

"Burn it to the ground," Brooke chimed in.

"Hello," Stan called out, still leaning against the barnwood fence. He pulled the red handkerchief out of his pocket and wiped the sweat from his well-tanned brow. Strong chin and six pack, he was nearly the opposite of Nate. Nate was good looking enough, and he went to the gym, worked on the elliptical to keep toned, but he was better suited to a city. He wasn't tanned, wasn't muscular or tough. Nate knew how to navigate heavily packed sidewalks, or where to get a latte no matter which street he was on. Stan looked like he just stepped out of a wilderness survival magazine.

"Hi," Nate said, stretching from the seven-hour drive. It had seemed like forever. He walked over to the fence and shook the hand of the smiling, muscular man. "I'm Nate. Werner's son."

"Werner's son? Nate! Yes, he talked about you. A lot. Before... you know. Damn, it's good to finally put a face to the name." Stan's grip was firm, eyes steel grey, his dark hair flowing down to his shoulders. "You lived in L.A., is that right?

"Yeah, moved out there when I was a kid."

"Old Werner told me that, too. I'm Stan, by the way. Been here nearly ten years now. Bought the house from the Hogarths. You know the Hogarths?"

Hogarths was a name well known in town. They'd owned some oil derricks, pulled in a good living, but they weren't oil barons by any means. They always thought the big score was just around the corner. Lloyd Hogarth spent his days driving from derrick to derrick, checking activity, ensuring everything was going smoothly. That much time alone in the desert does something to a man. Does something to his mind. One day he came home, packed up the house, and that was that. Sold the house through a broker, to Stan, apparently.

"Yeah, I knew Lloyd. Heard he..."

"I'm Brooke," Brooke butted in. The Pomeranian, finally released from her cage, yapped incessantly at Stan, who looked down at the little thing for a moment, then ignored it. Brooke thrust her hand into Stan's, eyes fixed on his. Stan shook her hand, pulling it in close.

"Hi, Brooke. Stan. So, are you here to make arrangements for the house?"

"Nope," Nate said, shifting uncomfortably, "we're moving in."

"Hallelujah!" Stan said, slightly too loud and boisterous for the occasion. "It'll be nice to have someone in this old house. Between my house and Beatrice across the way, this neighbourhood is starting to clear out. Wouldn't want to lose the town, you know? Such a great little town. Quiet, good people, you know? Not like living in an apartment building with a thousand strangers all around you. I've lived in crowded conditions, and let me tell you, after a while you crave the outdoors."

"Beatrice still lives across the street? Oh honey," Nate said, smiling, although Brooke didn't have her eyes on him, "Beatrice ran the library. I used to see her all the time. I can't believe she's still alive! She was old when I was a kid."

"You should visit her. She has a chicken coop behind her house and gives away free eggs."

"And what do you do?" Brooke asked.

"Reclamations. Retired young." It was hard to pinpoint Stan's age. He was older than Nate, certainly. Looked weathered but not wrinkled. Authoritative.

"Watch your dog," Stan said, smiling and turning back to his yard work, "we've had a few strange incidents around town. Coyotes, probably."

Nate walked up the three porch steps to the door. The key slipped into the keyhole smoothly, but turning it required some force. After wiggling the key for a moment, swearing, it gave, and the door creaked open. He stepped it, and behind him, Brooke ascended the rickety steps and set foot into her new home. The house smelled of dust and mildew. "So this is it,"

"I know it doesn't look like much," Nate said, but he wasn't really thinking of what he was saying. He wasn't thinking about Brooke, about the yapping dog or how his life was falling apart. He was transformed. He was ten years old, standing in the house. Nothing had changed. Sure, everything looked greyer, covered in a layer of dust from years of abandonment, but everything was in the same place. Same threadbare sofa, same pictures on the wall. Same mounted wolf's head from one of his father's many hunting trips.

And then it was like he was holding his mother's hand, backpack jammed with clothes, being yanked out of the house. He hadn't realized they were leaving for good. Hadn't said goodbye to his friends, although really, he didn't have any worth saying goodbye to. Just a backpack in one hand, getting dragged out to the car.

"Nate... Fuck," Brooke said, anger giving way to disbelief, "you can't expect us to live here. I mean, holy shit... Look at this place."

"We've lived in worse. It's a step back, I know, but we can do this. Look," he said, walking through the living room and into the kitchen, "we can set the kitchen up. We used to cook dinners. Remember? You'd make dough and we'd throw it in the air like a pizzeria? Those were good times. And look here." Nate pushed on the back door. It needed a quick shove to push back the accumulated sand and dirt that had drifted up behind it. The house was exactly on the outside edge of town, and the desert was beautiful with wide open space, reddish brown earth and the mountains in the distance. "It's good here," he said. He let go of the door, and it slammed shut on its own, latching shut. Crooked house.

"Uh. Jesus, Nate. The shit you get us into." Brooke walked out of the kitchen and out to the car to get her bag. Nate took in every little nuance, every little memory. Even the scratches on the kitchen doorframe, marking his height over the years. They stopped around the four-foot mark.

He walked up the staircase. It creaked in all the same spots, and his bedroom was right at the top of the stairs. It hadn't changed either. He wondered for a moment if his father kept it that way to remember him by, but upon reflection, it was more likely Werner cared so little about the house that he just ignored it. Nate breathed in the musty air of his old room. It was exactly as it was when they left. The bed had the same blanket on it, the same plush iguana named Iggy, the same aquatic themed wallpaper with sharks in the background that always gave Nate a general feeling of unease. Even the dartboard was there. His father bought him the dartboard for his sixth birthday. It had real darts, not one of those magnetic ones or suction cups, but real, sharp, pointy darts with plastic shafts. It seemed like a terribly dangerous gift for a six-year-old, but Werner was never much concerned with Nate's safety. The dartboard hung, darts still sticking out of it, and a circle of little holes in the wall all around it from all the times Nate missed. Even the books on the bookshelf were the same. Nate looked through them, and they had a dreamlike quality, like he remembered reading them, but couldn't quite remember what any of them were about. That was his general feeling about the whole place.

Brooke appeared in the doorway. She'd managed to get up the stairs and into the master bedroom while Nate was still mesmerized by the house.

"Bedroom smells like old man piss," she said.

4

Beatrice Hetherington peered out of her living room window. A car pulled into the Crossfield house. An unfamiliar car. She'd put down her tea and pulled herself from the brown Permacraft sofa, still crisp under the plastic protector after all these years. She carefully stepped up the stepladder to get a better view.

Beatrice Hetherington. Four foot nothing, would've been a recluse if the town didn't need a librarian. She looked a thousand years old but was closer to seventy. The tight bun in her hair might have been an alternative to a face lift, but it wasn't a good one. Some folks around town suspected she was a hoarder, one of those typical crazy cat ladies or obsessive collector of screeching parrots, but cats and birds were not her interest.

She'd had Rheumatic Fever as a child. It nearly killed her, as it did to a lot of kids back then. She'd survived, but it took its toll on her body, weakened her heart. She was always small, always more frail than the other children. For being the daughter of the mayor, she still had a hard life.

She could hear the commotion, the scratching from upstairs. "Shut up! I'm coming," she yelled, her voice weary from the years.

She carefully backed off of the stepladder, walked across the worn hardwood floor. She looked up at the portrait of her father, painted in oils. He looked sternly back at her, even after all these years. In front of the portrait was a gossip chair, the rotary telephone sitting on the attached table. The phone hadn't rung in years. Beatrice checked it now and then, just to make sure it was still working.

Beatrice walked everywhere around town, to work and back almost every day, and out for breakfast and church on Sundays. She never owned a car. Never had a need to, as the town was small enough to navigate on foot, and she'd never left Red Valley.

She walked through the kitchen and unlocked the door that lead up to the attic. Pausing a moment to look at the clock, she pondered for a moment. Then she turned back to the fridge and pulled the bucket from the bottom shelf. She jabbed her finger into the offal inside. It had thawed.

Bucket in one hand, she leaned on the rail for support, but walking up and down the steps to the attic ten times a day made it easier through routine. She pulled on the small chain on the bare lamp fixture attached to the rough wooden ceiling. There were boxes in the attic, a cast iron treadle sewing machine her mother used to use, and deep in the back of the attic, far enough away to still be in shadow, were the bars and bolt-locked cage door.

"New neighbours again. Like that man moving into the Hogarth house," Beatrice spat, disgust almost palpable. "What do you think, children? You like having new neighbours? You like having more people around?"

Screeching, like wild animals, teeth gnashing, was the response.

"All these hotshots from the city. Fancy cars and fancy clothes. Feh! They think they're better than us. That's the truth."

More screeching, huffing and snapping. The musky smell of damp fur in the air. There was no window to the attic. No one could see in, and Beatrice never had visitors. She picked up the metal bucket, filled with hunks of raw meat and entrails, and pulled out an especially bloody, plump fleshy piece of meat.

"You're hungry, aren't you, children?" she said, waving the chunk of flesh in front of the cage doors. Inside, claws scratched against wooden floorboards with excitement. "Of course you are," she sighed. "You always are."

Small hands, like children's' hands, except long, bony, callused, with long yellowed fingernails, chipped and splintered, reached through the cage and strained to get at the meat. Beatrice relented and allowed it to be snatched from her hand.

"There you go. Good boys, so beautiful. Mama loves you. Yes, she does." More hands reached through the cage, and Beatrice delicately and carefully handed over the rendered flesh hunks.

"Shit," Beatrice said, suddenly looking down at the bucket. "I forgot to add your damn vitamins. How can you grow up healthy and strong without your vitamins?"

As she walked down the stairs, the shrieks of hunger grew, the scratching and clawing at the bars, at the floor.

"Quit scratching at the floor!" she yelled up harshly at the creatures.

Then one small hand reached up, to the cheap hook and eye latch holding the cage together. Inside, the creature strained, its small, wrinkled arm struggling against the bars. It was close, so close, but then another arm reached out, longer than the first one, and it managed to snatch the handle of the metal bucket. It yanked the bucket, the blood, flesh, and entrails slopping onto the floor, spilling out into a bloody puddle of carrion. Then the thin, pale limbs stretched out from between the bars, scrambling to scoop up and devour the bloody viscera.

5

Downtown Red Valley was basically a couple of roads running parallel, and three cutting across them. In an effort to attract tourists back in the seventies, they fronted all the buildings to look like they were built at the turn of the century. Mayor Hetherington pushed that one through. The pharmacy was still independently run, not yet taken over by the corporations of the city, and the hardware store still had wooden floorboards from the thirties. There was a coffee shop, called The Lucky, had been around longer than anyone could remember, serving greasy diner eggs and burnt coffee. It was a single business in a line of attached brick storefronts. Next to it was the headquarters for The Real World Monitor.

Two stories tall, cracked plaster and rusted pipes, The Real World Monitor building contradicted its national syndication with its meagre office space. It had a sign above the door which read 'The Real World Monitor: We Print News Other Papers Dare Not.' The sign looked faded from forty years of the intense heat and light of a desert town. Brick supports barely held up the sagging ceiling over the open space on the second floor, crammed with desks and file cabinets.

The night hadn't been comfortable for Nate. Brooke fumed bitterly the whole time. Nate resigned himself to it, and they'd both made it an early night in the bed Werner used to sleep in. Brooke slept in, while Nate had made coffee by pouring boiling water through a coffee filter into his cup. Apparently, his father didn't have a coffee maker, or if he did, Nate couldn't find it. By the time he pulled up to the offices of the Real World Monitor, he was already on edge.

Nate remembered the building. As a kid, he didn't know what it was, never knew The Real World Monitor, or what news it was reporting. It had an air of mystery about it, like it was some religious thing, or one of those brainwashing cults run in secret, abducting people off the street and they'd end up selling flowers at the airport. Nobody ever seemed to go in or out of the building. He would've assumed it was out of business if he'd thought of it at all.

He parked the red Miata on the street, catching the eyes of a few locals sitting in the booths at the front of the Lucky. Red Valley didn't see many sports cars. Mostly pickup trucks and beaters.

Nate walked up to the glass and metal door of the office. The blinds behind the glass were stained and water damaged. It takes a lot to have water damage in the desert. He shoved the door, and it gave way begrudgingly.

Faces popped up from behind computers, seven or eight. They were all looking at him, not saying anything. Just looking. Astonished.

"Uh… I'm Nate…"

"Ooh! Scarface!" Mr. Leone said, coming out of his office. "Holy shit! You're Werner's kid! I didn't know if you were going to make it!" Mr. Leone had one of those mismatched bodies where the top half seemed to belong to a fat man and his bottom half to a skinny one. He wore jeans and an untucked white dress shirt, cowboy boots in the office. It was a contrast to Nate's suit and oxfords. Nate had dressed up for his first day, but apparently there wasn't a dress code among the journalists. Mr. Leone still had white powdered sugar on his moustache from his breakfast donut, beads of sweat on his forehead. He shook Nate's hand with agitation. "We only have a few people in the office here. Most of our reporters send their stories in. It'll be good to have you here. Hey! Let me show you around." He walked into the bowels of the office, his gait ungainly and clumsy, but he didn't seem to care. "Rant!" Mr. Leone yelled, startling an angry looking man.

"Fuck!" the angry man yelled, slamming his fist down on the keyboard of his computer. "What the hell, Leone! I was on a roll!"

"This is Nate. He's Werner's son. You remember Werner. Pulled that family out of that burning house way back when? Good guy."

The angry man stood up and both quickly and perfunctorily shook Nate's hand. "Mike Rant. I do editorials here." Rant was the only other person in the office wearing a suit, although his seemed too tight, especially around the collar. He had slick black hair and small, round glasses.

"This here is Dasha, author of 'Dear Dasha' and resident psychic," Mr. Leone said, pointing to a middle-aged African American woman wearing a purple head wrap. She looked up, a huge smile across her face.

"I remember you," she said, standing and wrapping her arms around Nate in a bear hug. Nate awkwardly hugged her back, feeling a sense of familiarity about the women, but unable to place her. He hadn't been a social kid. "You went to school with my brother. Moved away, right?"

"Yeah. Long time ago," Nate said, nodding at the woman. He had no idea who her brother was.

Mr. Leone continued leading Nate around the decrepit office, with its crumbling brick and dusty corners, spiders and cockroaches in a constant war for survival in the dark cracks in the walls. Nate was introduced to the nine men and women in total, all typing diligently away at their computers. He'd met an Argentinean journalist who was missing his two front teeth, a woman who called herself Xavianna, and five others whose names he'd already forgotten. The reminded him of worker bees, or maybe gophers. Or a combination of both. Each one had the same look in their eyes. They stopped caring years ago. No one talked to each other from their bare, characterless desks. Not even a family portrait anywhere to be found. For them, this was just another job, like they got the job when they were in their teens, and while unsuited to them, while never their dream job, they just seemed to forget that they were allowed to quit. Instead, they put their heads down and typed out their articles. Nine to five and nothing more.

"We haven't had a new employee here in years," Mr. Leone said, leaning his considerable bulk against a file cabinet, "lost a few on the way, but things have gone digital. You know how the world is. Never had someone from the city work here. Just locals, mostly."

Looking around, Nate couldn't imagine cramming more people into the small office, more desks and chairs, more empty lives and deserted dreams. "Well, deep down I guess I'm a local too. Just haven't been here for a while."

"Small towns always draw you home. Now, here's your desk," he said, wiping his hand across a wooden desk, red desert dust kicked up into the musty air, residue clinging to his hand. "Been awhile since this one been used. You know how to use a computer?"

Nate looked at the antiquated Apple Macintosh on the desk. Yellowed from years of use. Still had a floppy drive. "Yeah… but I don't know if I can use *that* one…"

"Ha ha!" Mr. Leone barked loudly, startling the other reporters. "Yeah, these old Macs are workhorses! They never break down, so we haven't needed to replace them. We use the word processing on them but take it easy on the internet. Costs money. We send the pictures off to Pronghorn Mesa, and they put everything together for us. It's a pretty sweet deal." Mr. Leone looked up and started sucking air between his teeth as if he was trying to get something unstuck.

"I appreciate this," Nate said, sitting down on his wooden chair, "I mean, after everything."

"What? That thing about the Mayor? The prison reports? Oh yeah, I guess a lot of papers wouldn't touch you after that mess! Ha ha! You don't worry about that here. We don't hold things like that against you. Ain't that right, Hardy?"

A skinny red-haired man at the next desk looked up from his fervent typing, laughed with a crooked smile. "Har har har!" Snaggle-toothed, threadbare green shirt.

"Well," Nate said sheepishly, "you can be sure that I won't do that again. After what it's done to my life, I learned my lesson."

"Stop right there, son," Mr. Leone said, putting his sweaty hand firmly on Nate's shoulder, "that's not what I'm saying here. See, the Real World Monitor, well, it ain't like those other newspapers. The news here comes fast and furious, and we don't spend a lot of time on all that fact-checking and confirming reliable sources bullshit. Maybe you have a dozen lawyers looking over your shoulder there in the city. We don't do that here. That's what I like about you, Nate. I like your ambitious side, boy. You're a spark plug."

"What..." Nate said, a look of disbelief crossing his face, "but this is a paper..."

"The Real World Monitor is a cutting edge paper," Mr. Leone bragged. He puffed his chest out, only putting more strain on the delicate buttons barely keeping his shirt on his massive frame. "No hidden agenda. No cover ups. We print news other papers dare not. It's written there on every issue. Did you hear about the infestation of Jewish vampires that were only repelled by the Star of David? No, course not. City papers wouldn't print that! How can you prove it? Bunch of chickenshits wouldn't print it, but we did. We did!

"Last week, some kid in Idaho threw a firecracker into an outhouse. You know kids. Little shits are always up to something. Anyway, this firecracker goes off and ignites all the methane down there. It was a deep hole, let me tell you. Explodes like you wouldn't believe. Two days later, in Pinehurst, it starts raining shit! I'm not fucking with you! That outhouse explosion blew the shit into the stratosphere and it rained down in a city! Ha ha! Now, you think the big papers want to talk about a whole town getting covered in fecal matter? Nope! Too distasteful. Too harsh for their namby-pamby readers. The Real World Monitor doesn't pull punches. We tell it like it is."

"I just don't want to be making things up..."

"Whoa whoa whoa! We don't talk like that here! No way," Mr. Leone looked like he was pretending to be insulted by the accusation. He hung his thumbs in his pockets of those skinny-legged jeans and turned down the corners of his mouth. "I never said we make stuff up. We take news leads, and I mean real news leads submitted by our readers, and write about them. Now, I have to be straight with you, we just don't have the resources to fact-check every little story, so we sometimes have to..." he paused, and raised an eyebrow thoughtfully, "creatively fill in the blanks, if you get my meaning. We don't have the manpower to ensure every story is one hundred percent legit, but I'm sure our readers are honest people. Make stuff up? Never. Right, Hardy?"

Hardy looked over, nodding, bottom lip stuck out.

Mr. Leone leaned in close, so close Nate could feel his hot breath on his cheek. "We got ourselves journalistic integrity here." He stood up, stuck out his impressive gut, and started walking back to his office. "Ain't that right, Hardy?" he yelled back over his shoulder.

"Har har har!"

"Dig through the mail pile and get down to it. Three stories a day, any less and we miss a deadline, and we never miss a deadline." Mr. Leone slammed the door to his office behind him yelling, "Good luck!"

Amid the click-clacks of the neighbouring computers, Nate booted up his own and looked in his desk drawers. Whoever used this desk last didn't clean anything out. It was stuffed with blunt pencils, dry pens, empty cigarette packs, and crumpled sticky notes. Nate spent his first half-hour cleaning out the desk, gathering supplies, and then, finally, walking to the letter pile. He flipped through a few of them, brow furrowed.

"Hardy... what... what is this crap?"

Hardy looked up, red hair uncombed and in need of styling. He just stared, mouth agape.

"Mr. Leone can't be serious about this! Look at this crap! Frog convicted of Murder? Vatican Mafia? Look at this one," Nate said, flapping the page in front of him. "Princess Di married John Belushi in top secret wedding. This is... this is bullshit!"

"Mmph," Hardy grunted, still looking up at Nate. Nate looked back, breath taken away, but saw little response from the red-haired reporter.

"Ah fuck this. I need some air," Nate said.

6

The hooded figure shuffled lightly through the dank, polished marble tunnels. The ketoret smoke, the incense offering to God, clung oppressively in the air, sweet and heavy, making breathing difficult in these already claustrophobic passageways. The figure bobbed and weaved throughout the corridors, occasionally spinning, as if somewhere in his subconscious music was playing, his footfalls in the silence the beat of his mental soundtrack. The tunnels were dark, so dark at times it was completely absent of light. Utter blackness. Finally, after he deftly predicted the corners and outcrops, candles on the floor gave a glimmer of light. Monks kept these candles lit, but given the state of things, even they were spread thin. Everyone could feel it. Something unmistakable, yet indefinable. A feeling of anticipation mixed with the sombre reality of his own impermanence on this world. Immortality isn't the right word. Not for him.

The signet door, one of the many holy doors hidden around the world, was secret, impassable to all except those especially chosen. Only pure, cleansed souls were allowed to enter. Or, those whose souls are untouchable, even by God himself.

Michael removed his hood to see more clearly in the flickering orange-yellow candlelight. His features were gaunt, sunken cheeks and pale skin. Thick black hair parted in the middle revealed a cross, deep in his forehead. Not a scar, but more like the flesh had been burned, melted away, leaving behind a perfect plus sign in his pale, nearly translucent skin. He lifted a delicate hand, thick golden ring on his middle finger. Pressing it against the sealed door with a tap that would've been inaudible except for the silence of these catacombs, the doors, fighting against the ancient hinges, slowly creaked open.

He had made it. He had arrived at Nestorian, the hidden subterranean city. The chamber was massive, stretching out for hundreds of miles in every direction, opulent in its golden filigree and baroque carvings on the marble walls and innumerable pillars, arches far, far above. Each arch depicted Angels, demons, pagans being eviscerated, dragons being slain by holy knights, and images of Jesus. Golden statues of Jesus reflected the infernus fires, piercing the smoke billowing from the censers that dangled from the darkened, unseen ceiling a thousand feet above. Hustling between these statues were boys. Young, wearing thick white ecclesiastical robes in the sweltering heat. Some polished the gold, carried stacks of silks, or followed behind bloated old priests who were lost in their own thoughts.

The holy city was littered with footpaths leading to acre-wide parks of golden pews or giant, jewel encrusted suits of armour, but in the centre of Nestorian, all was rendered inconsequential by the pyramid of gold, topped with a throne that would shame the wealthiest kings in history. Michael danced between these holy relics, his footwork graceful as he reached the pyramid and climbed the five hundred golden steps up to the throne.

Once he'd climbed the steps of the brilliantly gilded pyramid, Michael fell to his knees in front of a throne where a man sat, the shadows casting him in total darkness. Surrounding him, boys in thin nettle yarn robes, fanned him, massaged his shoulders, or simply polished the throne.

"Your holiness," Michael said, his voice effeminate, "it is time."

The man stood. The fires burning behind the throne cast him in complete silhouette, so as he stood, Michael could not make out his features. Michael had been in this room many times but had never had cause to address the man directly. Even throughout his life, meeting royalty and celebrity, Michael hadn't ever felt this kind of nervousness.

"Address me further, my Agnus Dei. Tell me of the signs and portents." His voice was old, cracked, but authoritative. Even through the darkness, Michael could feel those piercing eyes looking at him, possibly looking deep into his soul had he had one. No, Michael only had an echo of a soul, a reflection, protected by the cross melted into his forehead.

"Your holiness, it is as the scripture has spoken. The death of a seventh son by a two-headed snake, a rain of excrement, a man eviscerated by a rainbow, all of the predictions. Your holiness, it is time."

The man stepped forward, using a long golden sceptre to aid his aging body. He wore a cassock of white and gold with intricate red stitching, a fisherman's ring on his puffy finger. Michael looked up, finally glancing his form, studying him for the first time up close, instead of on balconies or photo opportunities. He was old, in his seventies, his sagging features indicative of his years of ease and opulence. He turned and paced a few steps. "Good... good," he said, a yellowed grin widening on his aged face. "Odd, I've felt no movement of the cartogram. It must be impending. Have the consecrated virgins monitor the wavelengths of ascension. Prepare the altar boys and my gestatorial chair for travel..."

Whack!

Pain shocked through Michael's head, or what approximated for pain now that he had crossed over. Holding his sceptre aggressively, the man prepared to hit him again.

"Avert your eyes!"

Michael smoothed his face where the sceptre had struck him. He stared down at the golden floor of the pyramid, ashamed.

"You have not earned the right to look upon my visage!"

"My apologies" Michael begged, making sure he didn't accidentally glance at the man's face again, "sorry your holiness! Please, please forgive me!"

"I am not one to forgive lightly," said the man, "I brought you into this life, and hand to God I can withdraw the favour. I have need of you, else your body would've been melted down for candles!"

"Forgive me… please…"

The man, jaw clenched, spat his words like scalpels. "Fetch my holy robes! Fetch my crosier! Alert your brethren! Alert the Tartak Cannibal Girls! Alert the Stigmatics and Abbadon's Locusts!"

"Of course… immediately, your holiness."

Two boys rushed to the man's side, and he rested his arms heavily across them as he stepped down from the throne, and then slowly stepping down the steps of the pyramid. Michael cowered behind him. "Finally. Decades have passed. My predecessors hoped for this privilege, but it has come to rest upon me. God has chosen wisely, and I will not allow myself to fail."

John waited at the bottom of the stairs. He, like Michael, had a cross stamped into his forehead, but John was not slight, not effeminate or pale. John had steel grey eyes, hair cut short on the sides, and wore a grey suit and tie beneath his white robes. "Well, your holiness, it looks like we got ourselves quite a fight on our hands," John said, his accent unmistakably Bostonian, each word enunciated clearly. He handed the man his papal robes, and his mitre, the tall pointed hat he wears for all of his papal duties.

"We do, Mr. Kennedy. We must prepare, for the time has come," the Pope said, face illuminated by the bonfires, "for the cleansing this world."

7

The Lucky in Red Valley is like any greasy spoon in any town in America. Booths and a counter, window to the kitchen where Old Don Watson spins the metal wheel to see the next order. No computer, but the cash register got upgraded to electric in the seventies.

"Adam and Eve on a log, blindfolded," Irma calls to Don, spinning the metal wheel, "you want coffee with that?" she asked Nate. Irma was in her fifties, married Don young, too young some people speculated. She started in the back, washing dishes, and after a few weeks was filling in shifts for the waitresses. Soon enough, the floor was hers, as was the chef.

"Yeah," Nate said, "black, please." Nate looked around the diner. It hadn't changed. Nate remembered the hot summer days when his father would bring him into the diner for a milkshake. Maybe he remembered it so well because it was a rare moment of tenderness from his father. The milkshake wasn't the kind you got in the city, paper cup and plastic straw. No, the milkshake came in a glass, and they gave you the metal mixing cup with it as a free refill. You could get a burger, or a deluxe burger for fifty cents more, and you'd know they'd hand-formed the patties in the back, bought the tomatoes and lettuce from local farmers. Even the buns came from the Medeiros' bakery that morning, not pre-packaged weeks ago. Nate hadn't hung around home in the morning, so breakfast had been the rushed cup of coffee and a peanut granola bar. Now, he had work on his mind. He had his future, his marriage, and his whole life on his mind.

"Hey, you Werner's boy?" Merle Winslow called over.

Nate looked up. "Yeah," he said, astonished to be recognized. It'd been decades. "I know you. I can't remember your name." Nate had been so focused on his own problems, he'd felt alone in the diner, but there they were. The same guys that had been there years and years ago. Seemed like they were there every time Nate's father brought him. There were others there, in the diner, young couple skipping school, old people with grandkids.

"Flop one with a mystery in the alley," Irma yelled after getting the order from a black soldier reading a wrestling magazine, duffle bag on the floor by her feet.

"Merle," he said by way of introduction. "You used to come 'round. I didn't recognise you, but Arland here, he's got an eye for faces and names. Knew you the moment you stepped in the door. Would've said something earlier, but it looks like you got something on your mind. Your pa all right?"

"The same. I'm going to see him today. I mean, not that he'd know it."

"Damn shame. Age is a sonofabitch, all right. Ain't that right, Arland?"

"Never done me no wrong," he said, smiling. Merle and Arland were the opposite ends of the spectrum, physically. Merle was short, squat, with a bushy white beard. He wore a lumberjack shirt in the middle of the summer heat. Arland, conversely, was tall and skinny. Both worked in the military before they closed the base. Most soldiers left, but Merle and Arland had met a few of the local girls, started up with them, and decided to stay. Merle had a strong back, and Arland had a memory that couldn't be met by anyone.

"I remember you guys from when I was a kid. It was like, you two would start a conversation, and soon Dad would be at your table, joining in, and then everyone in the place was part of the conversation. I never knew what you were talking about. I was too young. I was just here for the sundaes."

"Old enough now, I suppose," Merle said, slurping his coffee. "Pull up a chair."

Nate tossed the idea around in his head. Moping over his cup of coffee wasn't going to do him any good, and maybe talking to someone other than his wife, or Mr. Leone, would lift his spirits. So he picked up his cup and saucer and moved over.

"Thanks. It's been rough. Coming back isn't what I thought it would be. It's like, everything is a little weird here, know what I mean?"

"Town's always been weird," Arland chimed in, "it's a strange little town, I tell ya. Strange little desert town."

"It's not really all that weird, though," Nate said, sipping his coffee, "you know, it's like every town is a little weird. Like, Beatrice Hetherington and all those cats she used to have, half starved and hunting for rats in everyone's backyards. And that Bembenek boy, they used to warn me about him, said he was born differently because he couldn't talk or take care of himself, but sit him in front of a piano and suddenly he was Beethoven. I mean, it was a huge mystery at the time, but it's just Autism. We know it now. It's not weird at all. Nothing here is really weird. It just feels weird. Maybe it's just so different from the city, or maybe it's that I remember everything, but through the eyes of a ten-year-old."

Merle looked at Arland, a grin on his face, like he was met with a challenge. "Well, you live here long enough, you'll see how weird it is. Right, Arland? You got anything for him?"

"Weird stories? Well, there's Ambrose Bainbridge. That's a good one," Arland said. The name rang a bell for Nate, but he couldn't place it.

"Yeah," said Merle, "Ambrose and Isabelle. That was pretty weird."

Irma walked over, hot plate of basted eggs and sausage. "You're not listening to these old bullshitters, are you?" She put the plate down in front of Nate. The food looked great, with the side of hash browns actually fried potatoes, not frozen deep-fried garbage, although the red from the maraschino cherry bled into the orange slice on the garnish, and Nate wondered if he was supposed to eat it or save it for the next customer.

"Nineteen eighty-one," Arland started, leaning in, his back hunched as if he were telling his most sacred secret, "we all had a lot more hair back then, including Merle here."

"Mine just fell down my face!" Merle said, stroking his beard.

"Isabelle Halleywell was the prettiest girl in town. Only redhead around these parts, and eyes like Audrey Hepburn. All the boys around town were after her, rich boys, athletic boys. Hell, even some of the young dogfaces from the base had eyes on her. Not Merle and I though, too young, but none of them had a chance. See, she only had eyes for Ambrose Bainbridge."

"Fifteen years younger," Merle said, "and I'd of had a chance. Could've gotten turned down proper, like the rest of the town's boys."

"Don't you mind Merle. He's just lucky his wife has bad eyesight."

Nate dipped his toast slice into the runny yellow yolk of his eggs. He understood why his father always ended up at this table. They played off of each other perfectly, told the kinds of jokes dads tell each other. Nate was feeling decidedly grown up, sitting with these men, not exactly idols of his childhood, but definitely people he looked up to. Strangely, it felt like a rite of passage.

"Anyway, story has it that one night they went for a drive. Up to the park, the one with the hoodoos. If you remember correctly, ain't nothing good ever happen out at the hoodoos. Moonlight glistening off the dew is just too perfect, gets into a person. Lots of hasty marriages happened after visits to the hoodoos. Lots of babies nine months later, too," Arland said, giving Nate a quick nod and a wink, making a 'tck' sound to emphasize his point.

"And that Ambrose, well, maybe it was the moonlight, or maybe it was Isabelle's beautiful doe eyes, but he got himself all worked up. Got forward with Isabelle. Tried to take advantage before they were married, if you catch my drift. Well, Isabelle was Roman Catholic. They don't go for that. Next thing you know, Isabelle is buttoning up her shirt and slamming the car door with old Ambrose Bainbridge scrambling to get himself in order. Now get this, she starts walking for town. Figured walking for three hours was better than getting pawed at by Ambrose, and there's Ambrose following after her, begging and pleading for her to just get back into the car. But you know those redheads, fiery. She wasn't having anything to do with it. Ambrose figured he's lost his chance with her, and he starts yelling at her to get back in the car, and she starts yelling back. Out there in the middle of nowhere, nothing but the hoodoos to hear them.

"Now, they get arguing so much that they don't notice the light in the sky, and it weren't no helicopter. You see where this is going."

"No one saw Isabelle Halleywell again," Merle said, chipping in. "She was taken."

Nate looked at them, incredulously. "Didn't anyone suspect that maybe there weren't any aliens? That maybe the argument got away on Ambrose?"

"Oh, Ambrose was all sorts of broke up over it. Didn't talk about it much. Sure, police looked, search parties throughout the desert, the whole nine yards, but nothing. No proof of anything, except Ambrose's word that it was extraterrestrials."

"Ambrose left town not much later. Left the whole desert. Local police never laid off of him, although they couldn't put him in jail without something to make it stick. Living in a town where everyone thinks you maybe killed your girlfriend might just be jail enough for some. Word is he settled up north, in the mountains. Raises alpaca or something," Merle said, draining the last of his coffee from his cup.

They sat there for a moment, letting it sink in. Nate finishing up his eggs.

"I don't know, guys. Yeah, it's weird, but explainable. Everything is explainable when you get down to it. Everything weird is just coincidence, or bullshit. This Ambrose guy, there's more to it than just little green men latching onto his girlfriend. Something happened to her, sure, but I'm just not buying it was extraterrestrial."

Arland reached across the table, his considerable hand grabbing Nate by the shoulder. "You wait. Few months here, that'll be nothing."

8

The movers had come. The cramped house was full of taped-up boxes, some half opened and emptied as Brooke attempted to regain some sense of normality in her life in this alien environment. Her eternity floor lamp, a thousand dollars from Currey and Company, was propped up haphazardly against the wall. The Areca palm was looking dry and dying, but at least the Caesalpinia Bird of Paradise plant fared better, better even than it had in the city. She wasn't from the desert. She was from Seattle, lived with the tall trees, thick forests, moss everywhere. They didn't have to worry about feeling drained by the lack of humidity in the air. To the contrary, the air was so moist they had to wash the window sills with bleach to prevent mould. Then her father got transferred. Lost all her friends, lost the forests and the ocean salt in the air, and came to the dry pavement and monolithic buildings of Los Angeles. Then, worse, Red Valley.

She'd felt alienated before. She'd been the new girl at school, the one who didn't fit in. Brooke Lundsford, then, had been labelled a hippie chick, and instead of fighting against the outdated label, chose to embrace the title. In high school, she'd grown her hair down to her hips, wore whatever floral prints she could get a hold of, and started a spiritual journey into the new age movement. She'd found a book that would tell you which crystals would bring you happiness, love, money, and enlightenment. Then she searched out more and more, sitting in coffee shops reading books on how water droplets would change their molecular structure when spoken to harshly or with love, books about chakras, acupuncture points, or how to entice a lover by burning rosemary incense in the bedroom. Maybe her sense of magic is what first appealed to Nate, but people change and grow, and Brooke went from thrift store shopping to high fashion and power suits, from their first bachelor suite above the fish market to the fourteenth floor in a four bedroom, striving for more and more, dreaming of the penthouse suite. When her shelter cat sneaked by the concierge and went missing, she settled on a purebred Pomeranian with papers.

Then, uprooted again, she found herself in Red Valley.

Still, through all the frustration, all the disappointment, and through Toodles incessant barking, she was trying to make the best of it. Toodles wasn't happy. Neither was Brooke.

But the heat of the day did finally give way to the night, and the to the cool breeze of the desert. Nate had come home from his first day late, only to find a mound of his father's furniture in the front yard. It was the furniture he'd grown up with. Even his old bed was out there, the blanket he used when he was just a kid. His father was not one to change anything. Now the brown threadbare davenport was sideways in the driveway while their white B&B Italia sofa and chaise took its place. All the family photos and cheap garage sale prints of famous paintings spread out in the dirt. Last night's uncomfortable sleep in Werner's bed, the strange scents of the elderly man, were replaced by their own king size Hastens, satin sheets and ergonomic pillows.

Dinner had been quick and hasty, eating pasta boiled on the chipped and dented old coil stove with canned sauce heated up in their $1200 Elite microwave. Their last oven stayed with the apartment, so this one would have to be replaced. There was no delivery in Red Valley either. Dinner in the city was usually either out with friends or colleagues, or sushi, never pizza, ordered in. There was this great little Italian place a few blocks from their apartment that had a linguini aglio e olio that was Brooke's favourite. They'd get dressed up, as in the city they'd never go out to a restaurant wearing what they'd worn to work, or, God forbid, jeans and a t-shirt. It was an event. They'd get dressed up, order wine, and Brooke would get the linguini. It came with an additional basket of fresh buns, as there was so much oil one could sop up the mixture with the bread and still have more than enough to coat the freshly made pasta. Candlelight, black tablecloths, violinist.

As far as Brooke could tell, Red Valley had a cafe in the gas station and a little greasy spoon Nate mentioned was beside the Real World Monitor building. The Lucky. Linguini aglio e olio was long gone.

Nate lay in bed that night, reading through back issues of The Real World Monitor, although his mind kept returning to the fact that there they were, in his old house, in his parents' bedroom. It was always his father's house, back then, never his mother's, even though she was the one who raised Nate while his father was stuck at the military base, days, weeks on end. They wouldn't see Werner, and then suddenly he'd be there, maybe paler from being stuck in offices all day, sometimes stressed out and exhausted from the long hours. Nate's mother should've welcomed these times, for raising Nate wasn't easy, and she was basically a single mother most of the time, but Werner was far from supportive, and even when living his own house, he never really came home.

It wasn't that Nate was a bad kid. He was fine, nondescript, an average student with good grades who liked to stay in at recess and talk to the teacher rather than run around with his peers. At home his room was clean, his few chores of washing the dishes and sweeping the sidewalks were always done without grumbling. At that age he was still too young to sneak out with girls or underage drinking. He did, however, have a penchant for sneaking down the stairs to watch television late in the night after everyone had gone to bed.

That was his vice. Westerns, monster movies, gangster films, whatever was on the late movie from midnight to three. The censorship was lax after midnight, and he remembers hearing adults swearing in the movies, bare breasts and bedroom scenes, bloody gunfights and gore. Afterwards, he'd sneak back to bed, aroused from the nudity or scared from the ghost stories, and coax himself back to sleep. His parents had tried to figure out why his teachers were telling them that he was always falling asleep at his desk.

"So I'm supposed to write three stories a day, and I don't have a problem with that," Nate said that night, finally resting after the long day. He was flipping through back issues of the Real World Monitor while Brooke swiped across articles from the fashion magazines she had downloaded, pausing every so often to lavish affection upon Toodles. So far Nate had discovered that Nancy Reagan had been a robot, undersea crab men were on the internet luring women to the sea to mate with, and that there was absolutely nothing worth reading in the entire stupid excuse for a newspaper. "The problem I have is that it's like, I have to pretend that I actually believe this crap! Mr. Leone was talking to me with a half smirk the entire time, basically telling me that they only hired me because they thought I could make this stuff up."

"You did make stuff up."

Brooke's words cut. Cut deep. He stopped reading the article. He'd flipped over the more vulgar ones, like the woman who had her breasts enlarged until they were bigger than a bus. He also skipped the ones that were obvious right-wing propaganda, like Mark Rant's ridiculous editorials where he used terms like Feminazi, adding in pictures of feminists as women with swastika tattoos and jack boots. He'd ended up reading an article about a man in Uruguay who was cut in half by a rainbow as he was attempting to steal the treasure at the end. It was true that Nate made things up, but his lies weren't even close to writing about killer rainbows.

"Yes. I did. But you know damn well that I was right. The mayor was getting kickbacks from the prison, and no one was saying a damn thing. So I amalgamated a few people and made them a source. Nothing that I said wasn't true. Except…"

"Yeah, except you made up a source and implicated your boss, for fuck's sake."

Toodles suddenly jumped up from her resting spot, barking like crazy. The little fuzzy creature's yips and yowls were piercing.

"Toodles! Shut up!" Brooke yelled. "She's doing it again, Nate!"

"Yeah! I can hear it!"

"You said last night was just the first night in an unfamiliar house. This is the second night, and we have all our own stuff here now. It should be familiar to her. Do something!"

"Fine," Nate said, jaw stuck out with the day's frustrations. He grabbed the yappy little dog's mouth and held it closed. "Shut the fuck up!" He looked into the dog's eyes, attempting to intimidate the dog, but the sudden silence was broken by a scratching noise. It was coming from outside the house, like something was scratching on the walls.

"Shit," Brooke said, "it's that scratching. I thought I heard that last night, but I figured it was only a dream or something."

"Shhh," Nate hushed. He listened closely for a moment at the scratching. "It could just be some of the furniture leaning against the house. Rats maybe?"

"Yeah, you bring me to a fucking shithole town to a house with rats infesting the walls. Beautiful. You're such a good husband. Christ."

Nate let go of Toodles, who immediately resumed yipping and barking, running in circles on the bed sheets. He stood up, wearing only his striped boxer-briefs, and looked at the boxes. "I'll go look. Do you know where the flashlight is?"

"Yes, because I memorized every single thing in our apartment and which box the movers put them into."

Nate walked down the rickety staircase. He'd done it throughout his childhood, until he went to the city. He remembered counting the steps, the turns, which floorboards creaked and where it was safe to start making noise, far from earshot of his sleeping parents, terrified that his father would wake up and catch him. Werner's punishments often outweighed Nate's crimes.

Scratching at the back door. Nate stiffened.

Toodles wouldn't let up on her barking, but Nate manoeuvred through the boxes, slapped his hand along the walls until he remembered where the light switches were, and finally found himself at door to the back porch. He turned on the back light to the sound of skittering claws. He paused a moment, a chill running through him, for the sound was definitely an animal of some sort, or animals. He picked Toodles up under his arm to prevent her from bolting out the open door and steeled himself.

Nate threw open the door. "Who's there!" he yelled out into the emptiness. He looked out into the blackness of the night, the back yard that stretched out into desert, the void of nothingness that lingered in front of him.

9

The desert holds many things. Skeletons never to be found, creatures yet undiscovered, and a shack. Maybe it's a geological illusion, like magnetic hills, or maybe it's something more, but the shack is in plain view, but never seen, never noticed. If you were searching for it, you would walk right by, and by some trick or impulse, you'd miss it. But Colonel Nine knew where it was.

"So, it's a shack?" Phaedra asked from the passenger seat of the Jeep, loud enough to be heard over the static of the radio, which Colonel Nine was playing loudly for no reason that Phaedra could discern. Corporal Phaedra Wilson hadn't been given much information. Wasn't anything new for her. The military wasn't as bad to African Americans, nor to women, as they had been in the past. There was still racism, even some systemic, but knowing what her father had gone through in Iraq, or her grandfather in World War 2, she knew she had it good. The problem for her wasn't the racism, or the 'old boy's club' mentality of the older officers towards a young woman in the ranks. It was her complete and utter lack of luck. You could be sure that if something bad were to happen, it would happen to Phaedra, first and worst. Even at a young age, she'd never won anything by chance. When she was in the school wrestling club, she'd lose, not because of lack of skill, which she had plenty, but some random element would conspire to ruin her plans. Be it a loose shoelace wrapping her ankles together or a fluorescent bulb in the locker room falling on her head before the meet so that she had to get stitches instead of competing, Phaedra always ended up with the short end of the stick. It didn't end in school, either. In the military, she'd always gotten the worst posts, the worst assignments, of anyone. She'd be the one stuck plucking bloated bodies from a swamp or guarding a decommissioned secret submarine base in Alaska in the dead of winter. Her last assignment was the leak in a secret military reactor. That one had consequences.

"Not just a shack, soldier," Colonel Nine said, eyes squinting behind the reflective lenses of his aviator sunglasses, "your post."

The Jeep sped through the barren land, no road, just avoiding the boulders, the creosote bush and California juniper, climbing over the rocky hills and along the trenches cut into the land by the scarce rains. Phaedra bounced around in her seat, sometimes clinging to the seatbelt to keep her thin body from being ejected entirely. Colonel Nine didn't have this problem. It had been two hours of driving through the rocky desert terrain, and Colonel Nine spoke little. Phaedra knew better than to ask questions, so she sat and retained her thoughts. At least she'd had a day off in the small nearby town the day before. Managed to have a breakfast in a greasy spoon, pick up a few vintage wrestling magazines and two books from a dusty old bookshop. Even the night in a hotel rather than a military cot was a nice change. It felt like home, even though it'd been years since she'd had a real home.

"Got it!" Colonel Nine exclaimed sharply, turning the wheel with a jerk that snapped Phaedra out of her thoughts. "Sucker's a pain in the ass to find out here."

The Jeep pulled up to the shack. No bigger than a one-car garage, thrown together from spare lumber and rusty nails, the shack was barely standing. An array of solar panels laid out beside it was hooked to a couple car batteries, and an orange extension cord snaked inside. A stone's throw away from the shack was the MGPTS, the Modular General Purpose Tent System, where Phaedra would be stationed. Most people just called it a tent. Had a couple of chairs out front. Fire pit for warmth at night, tanks of water to survive.

"But this post... it's just this shed, right?" Phaedra finally asked. The military had asked her to do some strange things in the past, things Phaedra knew not to question, but a pile of boards in the middle of nowhere was confusing.

"Not a shed either," Colonel Nine said, hoisting his brawny but aged body out of the Jeep, "this here is a very important military base. It don't look like much, I can see that, but it is, sure as shit."

"I've heard what happened to the last guy that was here," Phaedra said, hesitantly. Gossip wasn't tolerated in the military, but when you mentioned to your bunkmates where you were headed, it was hard not to talk about it. Worse when the last guy was driven to suicide.

"Oh, that. Damn shame. Good soldier, no doubt, but his mind was weak. The desert isn't easy, and due to the secret nature of this site, we don't want to fly out here. Soldier or two passing through town isn't anything to worry about, especially with the retired base just outside of Red Valley. Helicopters and squads are a different story. Military isn't known for a soft touch, but this one, well, it needs subtlety.

"But you," he continued, walking up to the shack and spitting on the ground, "you're different. You've had it tough and you made it. You kept your composure at the nuclear site, and we noticed. You've got grit. You'll do fine out here.

"What are my orders, sir?"

"No one gets in the shack. That's it. Someone tries, someone dies. Best it not be you." Colonel Nine turned his back on the decrepit shack and started walking to the Jeep, sweat already dripping down his crew-cut. Colonel Nine was a large man, sure, but he was fit. Beneath the extra pounds was muscle and a strong frame. His stomach didn't jiggle and wobble when he walked but was firm, still stuck out in front of him. His nose was red and visibly veined, salt and peppered moustache cropped sharply, and his greenish grey eyes beneath those reflective lenses were keen and piercing. "Satellite phone in the tent. Don't use it. The airways aren't safe. Hell, probably wouldn't work if you tried. Sunspots. There's also a small fridge in there that you can use to can keep your water supply cool and freeze your ice packs. Boil your rations over a fire. Hell, it's like you're on a camping trip. Just keep your eyes open."

"I don't go in the shack?" Phaedra said, pulling her duffel bag from the back seat of the Jeep. "I just watch it?"

"No one gets in. Someone tries, someone dies." Colonel Nine leaned into the Jeep and lifted the M16 rifle in its bag from the back. "Keep your weapon handy at all times. Keep her clean, lots of oil. Desert dust is a fucker on these things." He handed Phaedra the bag but didn't let go as Phaedra grabbed it. Instead, he leaned in close, as if telling a secret. "Desert is hard on the mind, girl," he said, voice low and rough. "People see things. They hear voices. Feel things that aren't real. Trust me, I've been here longer than you can imagine. Sat here in the desert, just like all the others who've done this post. Seen things… well, desert plays tricks on your mind. That's it. Prepare your mind, soldier. Keep yourself strong. Don't give in."

Colonel Nine pulled himself in and wrestled the key until the engine growled into life. "God be with you, soldier," he said as he let loose the clutch and pulled away, off into the desert.

Phaedra stood there. Backpack over her shoulder, gun in hand, alone in the emptiness of the desert. She stood and watched as Colonel Nine's Jeep went from full view to a mere trail of dust in the air, and finally off the horizon into nothingness. She was alone. Supposed to be a week until she was picked up, but she knew the military. A week could turn into a month without a second thought. Phaedra wondered how long the last guy had been at the shack.

The military hadn't been the first professional choice for Phaedra. Sure, it had always been an option, with generations of soldiers behind her, and three brothers already serving, but Phaedra had always had dreams. She'd run them through her head, like she did as she unpacked her pack, set up in the tent and put her sheet and blanket on the small cot. She'd wanted to be a professional wrestler. Not an Olympic wrestler, but the guys on television every Saturday afternoon, with their bright costumes and their outrageous moves. Brock Temper, Buckshot Kid, Jack "Voodoo" Allan. Joining them was her dream. She would practice with her brothers in the backyard, trying to bounce off of the chain link fence as if it were the ropes of the ring, climbing up them and leaping off onto the grass. Even in the high school wrestling club she'd been practicing the suplexes and more exciting moves, rather than the more effective arm drags and tie ups. Moves like the powerslam, piledriver, or brainbuster were kept for when the coach wasn't around, and the other teens were horsing around.

As the sun went down, Phaedra sat by the fire she'd made from the desert grasses and dry branches of the desert trees. The awkwardly jointed lengths of wood, smaller branches spreading out like broken fingers, along with the military fire starter packs, which were part of her supplies in the tent, made it easy to start a blazing bonfire. She was still daydreaming about the wrestling matches she'd seen when the traveling show would come to town, like when Osama Akbar fought Samson "American Dream" Steele and choked him unconscious with the American flag, or when Ripsaw Mulligan pulled the mask off of the Red Serpent, revealing that the villainous Serpent was actually Dapper Dennis Goodman. Of course, he'd been hypnotized by Chi Chang, the Chinese Cobra. And as dusk turned to night, the darkness engulfed all, except the small bedside lamp inside the tent, the smouldering fire, the light escaping inside the shack, and, of course, the glow of Phaedra's irradiated skeleton, glowing through her skin and into the desert night.

10

The night passed, fitfully. Toodles, the Pomeranian, spent a few hours under the bed, interspersing growling and whimpering. Nate woke at every growl, every whimper, wondering if whatever was scratching at the walls of their desert home had somehow made it inside. Finally, after hours of growling, Toodles relented, cozying up to Brooke, nuzzling her way under Brooke's arm and finally calming.

But it was stupid. He kept telling himself that over and over again. The desert was full of animals, dozens of which could've been making that sound. Weird little lizards, dozens of species of bats, rats, even neighbourhood cats. Sure, it might have been coyotes, but Nate didn't ever remember them coming into town. They kept to themselves, mostly, far outside of the sparse civilization of town. Whatever it was, though, had unnerved him, and his sleep was brief and uncomfortable. By the morning, he was so exhausted he barely noticed Brooke getting out of bed.

She, conversely, slept like a log. In the past couple of days she'd named off dozens upon dozens of reasons why the small town was detestable, but with the lack of any traffic sounds at night, and nearly complete darkness she slept more peacefully than she ever did in the city. She also woke with the sunrise, which she hadn't done in years. Not since those first few bohemian years with Nate, eating kale salads for supper and working at small independent coffee shops that served lattes in a bowl rather than a cup.

"Brooke?" Nate called, finally rousing himself from the few good hours of sleep that he had managed to sneak in. He rolled over, summoning all the strength he had just to pull himself out of bed, neck kinked from the stressful sleep behind him. He threw on yesterday's v-neck and shuffled his way down the stairs to the kitchen. He hoped Brooke put the coffee on. She hadn't.

"Brooke?" he called again. The house itself was comparable to the size of their luxury apartment in the city, it's single fourteenth-floor square footage equalling both floors of the house Nate grew up in, so there were few places that Brooke could be and not hear his voice. The basement was nothing more than a dugout, and the laundry room was at the back door, attached to the kitchen.

But the front door was open.

Nate stuck his head out the front door, suddenly awake with the cool air of the morning. He saw why Brooke hadn't heard him.

She was leaning up against the fence, talking with the neighbour, Stan. Robe open, showing her expensive negligee and cleavage. Her blond hair had a tousled look. She was throwing herself at him. Nate saw that. It wasn't the first time he'd seen her do that.

Stan was leaning on the fence too. His perfect black hair, his perfect teeth and strong jawline. He was wearing a shirt today, but the thin plaid western shirt did nothing to hide his muscular physique. The coffee cup in his hand was steaming.

"Brooke!" Nate said, louder than he'd intended. "I was wondering where you'd gotten to."

"Oh, hey Nate! I just came out here for the paper, and I saw Stan on his porch. Did you know Stan does carpentry on the side?" Brooke was doing her girly act.

"Morning, Nate," Stan said. "Not carpentry. Just a little woodworking. You know how it is. Start with a few household projects, and the next thing you know you're dreaming about building your own porch, or an armoire for the bedroom. These old houses have terribly small closets. Ah, I can see you know how these house projects go, one thing leading to another."

"Yeah," Nate lied. His experience with hammers ended at putting up a picture hook. He didn't own a screwdriver or drill, didn't shop at the stores where you need to assemble your own furniture. It was easier to spend his time doing things he was good at and pay someone else to do the things he wasn't. Sadly, he'd thought that the things he was good at involved writing actual news, getting hired by the country's most successful news television program and rising quickly to become the most respected journalist in the city. Turned out, he wasn't much more than a hack who'd let the pressure of success turn him into a liar. "I don't mean to break up your breakfast party, but I'm going to need to steal Brooke away for a minute."

"See you later, Stan," she said. Nate didn't see her wink, but he was sure she did.

Inside, the air became decidedly frigid. "What the fuck was that about?" Nate said the moment the door closed behind them.

"Oh god, what is your problem now? I can't even talk to the neighbours now?"

"You know exactly what I'm talking about. You were flirting with him."

"I'm just trying to make the best of this fucking shitty situation that your sorry ass landed us in! I'm not here to babysit your insecurities, you know! I'm barely hanging on, and now you're accusing me of flirting?"

"I'm not going through this again! Last time I forgave you! I should've left after what you put me through, but I stayed!"

"Oh, here comes the broken record. Yes, it happened. You said we'd put it behind us. But no, first time I start making a friend in this hellhole, you're all 'my wife cheated on me once' and I'm supposed to lock myself in a closet for the rest of my life."

She could've said more. Two years had passed since the staff party. She'd been drinking, and Nate had spent the whole night networking. He'd been off chatting with the network execs, the bosses who had heard about this new up-and-coming reporter who'd broken stories that no one had managed to get a foothold in. He'd been working a lot. He'd taken on a few large corporations, gotten enough dirt on them that they could air a piece on them without getting sued. He'd taken on a mafia family, corruption in the police force, and a dog fighting ring that included a local religious leader and four members of city council. He was taking on people of power, and his bosses noticed. It was the perfect time for him to make those connections and finalize his transition into prime time reporting. He'd noticed that she'd been drinking too much, which wasn't normally a problem for Brooke, but it took a while before he'd noticed that she wasn't at the table with the other spouses. He'd started wandering the halls of the convention centre, left the cacophony of laughter and chit-chat into the cool silence of the halls. The lights were dimmer, windows open to let a breeze through. Nate hadn't noticed how hot he'd gotten in the hall. Brooke couldn't be out in the hallway, he'd decided, but the cool breeze of the evening was nice. He looked out the window, the lights of the city, silhouetted buildings, sparks of headlights zipping in grid patterns across the overpasses, stopping and starting on the command of the traffic lights. He'd done well. He'd talked to the right people, mentioned the stories he'd written that had been aired, dropped the idea in the right ears that he should be on camera full time, and everything was on track. One year, he'd thought, and Mordechai Dantzig would have to retire. The man was pushing eighty. Nate would position himself as the newest up-and-comer, use his fan base to propel him into being the anchor, and then his life would be set.

Then he saw the vice president coming out of a storage closet.

"I don't know who that woman is," the vice-president whispered in his ear, slapping him on the back at the same time, "but you want to get a piece of it." Nate swore there was a stench about him, a foulness that permeated every pore of the man, but that might just have been the memory coloured by the situation, a symbol that perfectly exemplified the man, filthy, reeking, yet untouchable.

Then his life, for a moment, became a slow motion film, opening the door, Brooke pulling her panties up under her dress, lipstick smeared. The rage rising in him, the fury, the betrayal. He remembered that it was hard to think, hard to speak, hard to breathe. He didn't yell at her, instead just stumbled backwards as if being hit in the chest by a shotgun.

He'd forgiven her, it took months and months of therapy, certainly, but it never left him. The memory stayed fresh, image appearing in his thoughts when life got stressful, anger still deep beneath his skin. The anger was welling up, giving him tunnel vision. The words unable to form through the intensity of the rage. He'd wanted to let it all out, but could only manage a few words.

"We don't even get the paper!"

11

The emptiness, the vast expanse of nothing from horizon to horizon, the silence only broken by the occasional desert bird or the jolting hum of Phaedra's solar powered refrigerator kicking in.

Silence. It was not something Phaedra was used to.

Phaedra grew up in a busy household. Seven children. All boys except her. Phaedra was fourth, so she was exactly in the middle. Three older brothers to boss her around, blame her for the things they did, beat on her when she got too annoying, and three younger brothers to have to be responsible for when they broke things. Phaedra, in the middle, got the worst of it all, but that always did seem her lot in life.

Phaedra looked around the desert, laid out before her like an empty plate. Rocky outcroppings here and there, desert plants, but more than anything the most prevailing feature was simply the nothingness, the emptiness.

Then a whisper on the winds. One word. 'Help.'

Phaedra bolted upright from the wooden military chair she'd dragged into the shade of the tent, scanned the horizon. She widened her eyes in an attempt to see more clearly, but it was the same scene as before, the nothingness, the stark features and cloudless sky.

She wondered if she'd heard it at all. The mind plays tricks on a person when lacking stimulus. She'd read that. Still, she considered racing out into the desert to find the person, possibly save them from dying. She didn't. She convinced herself that it was in her mind. Tricks of the desert.

'Phaedra.'

Her name. Called once. It was no longer the voice of some distressed desert traveler or the random echoes of bird calls, but it almost sounded like her long dead grandfather. It was her mind, she was certain. It couldn't be the voice of her grandfather. He survived World War 2, was awarded the bronze star. Cancer took him in his seventies. She knew his voice, but it was impossible.

'Phaedra.'

Then, for just a moment, she thought it might have come from the shack.

The shack. Standing there only barely. Light still spilling through the gaps in the cracked boards, extension cord attached to the car batteries, powered by the few solar panels laid out in no discernable pattern.

Phaedra's household also consisted of her mother and father, and her widowed grandmother. Her father retired from the military when Phaedra was still in diapers. He'd still done security work from time to time, once being a bodyguard for Muhammad Ali. "Too much time away from my boys," he'd told the family, "they need a strong role model." It always felt awkward, like he had been talking to all the other children, but not her. It was as if her father didn't want to be her role model, but like it or not, he was. Her mother worked too, selling real estate, and was the breadwinner of the family. She was successful in real estate because she had a trustworthy face. That was one thing that Phaedra inherited from her that worked in her favour. She and her brothers were mostly raised by their grandmother. She always seemed like she was a hundred years old to them, bad vision, poor hearing, but she loved them. It was good. Noisy, but good. Raised them to be church-going children. Her mother never went, blamed it on her real estate business, because apparently Sunday morning is a hot time for people to buy houses. Her father only went because he'd always been made to go. It was never on his own accord.

Phaedra walked the perimeter of her post once an hour. No one had told her to do it, but there was nothing else to do. In between patrols she exercised, read her wrestling magazines, stoked her fire, shined her boots, maybe made a meal. Time was hard to keep track of out in the desert, so the patrols helped define her waking hours.

Wrestling. That was family time for Phaedra's family. Television would come on Saturday afternoons, and while her father normally shooed the boys outside every chance he got, Saturday afternoons had three different wrestling leagues, and they watched them all. Four hours, six boys, Phaedra, and their father, watching the countrywide league, an hour of recaps and interviews, then the smaller, local league, and finally the Mexican wrestling hour. The Mexican wrestlers were Phaedra's favourites, with their wild aerial stunts and their colourful masks. She learned more Spanish from the Mexican wrestling hour than she did in all of her years in school. Their Grandmother would bring out lunch, kids eating on the floor, and she'd stand and watch for a while. If Phaedra's mother were around, she'd disappear. She didn't understand it. She didn't get the allure of large men pretending to fight each other, scripted twists and turns, fake blood capsules and referees who acted like they were distracted when one would pull a pair of knuckle dusters out of his trunks to beat the other one with. Still, Phaedra's mother knew that it was quality time with their father, and she got quiet time to read. The only downside was that for the rest of the evening, the kids would be outside, re-enacting a somersault leg drop, or a corner slingshot splash, or whatever move the hero of the day pulled off in the ring, and inevitably one of them would come running in, crying, needing a bandage or just some comforting from their mother.

By late in the day, she noticed things appearing in the corners of her eyes. Shadows, desert animals, she suspected, but when she turned to see what it was, they were gone. Illusions. Nine had warned her to keep her mind strong, but it was difficult, even after these short days.

Then something stranger happened. Not just a hollow voice on the dry breeze, but something visible. Shimmering. Nearly imperceptible at first, like an outline of something that was drawn lightly and then erased. Phaedra squinted to try to discern the image in the brightness of the early evening sky. She thought it might be a swarm of small insects which wouldn't have surprised her as she'd expected bugs in the desert, although she hadn't seen many. As she thought about it, she realized that she hadn't seen any.

But it was more than just the outline. Tints in the air, silvers, golds, subtle, fog-like and ephemeral. Growing and fading. She wondered if it was simply refracted light of the evening sun or a desert version of the Northern Lights. Phaedra stepped closer to the shack, kept her eyes on the strange swirls above it. Slowly, shapes became more apparent. It almost seemed as though there was a head and a thick body, still just an outline, but the rough shapes of them. Phaedra's mind raced, from the ghost of her long dead grandfather to angels and spacemen. She couldn't figure out what the shape was, but whatever it was, every passing second it grew in form, and terrified her. She fought the urge to run, to hide under her bunk and force her eyes closed. The satellite phone in her tent suddenly seemed like a much better option, but she wasn't to use it, wasn't to jeopardize the site. Options were becoming increasingly scarce.

Schwaff! The sleek reddish rock left her deft fingers and cut through the mirage like a knife. The image quickly faded and dissipated. Phaedra threw another, just for good measure, but it was gone. She exhaled a deep breath, rationalized that it was really most likely a swarm of insects, possibly attracted to whatever was inside of that shack, and smiled at her own foolishness. Colonel Nine was right. The desert plays tricks on a person's minds, and she would have to be strong or else she'd start believing it.

So she did what she was out there to do. A quick patrol of the area, weapon in hand, walking around the outer edge of the site, and then another, in close to the shack.

But rounding the back of the shack, she stopped. At her foot lay one lone white feather, long and tapered, unlike any of the desert birds she'd seen. She kicked at it with her toe, then simply backed away, leaving it there to be carried away by the cool evening breezes.

12

The red Miata, dulled slightly from the long drive through the dusty desert, and a couple days away from the parking garage beneath the tall building they'd lived in when still in the city, pulled up to the Ancient Oaks Retirement Village and Convalescent Home. It was part of the town's only retirement home, and the elderly who were transferred into the convalescent wing rarely returned. Still, they made the home comfortable for the patrons. Bingo three nights a week, and Jed Haversome would come with his fiddle on Saturday nights to play for them. Movie night was on Tuesdays when they would play old black and white films. The convalescent wing was all locked. There were only five rooms, two nurses and one orderly in the wing. The town doctor, Dr. Bhijani, would come around every day to check in on them, but it wasn't his main concern. He had an office to run, but this month he was gone on vacation, so if there was trouble, Dr. Creakie would have to drive in from Pronghorn Mesa.

Werner Crossfield lived in the convalescent wing. He'd lived on his own until his condition worsened to the point where he'd get dressed in the middle of the night and try to break into the grocery store, or wander out into the desert, lost in time as well as in space. Then came the stroke, and that was it.

"Nate Crossfield," Nate said to the nurse at the doors. He pulled out his driver's license to show her. He'd managed to pull on a pair of pants before he left the house, still furious with Brooke. Shoes on, but no socks, and still wearing yesterday's v-neck t-shirt.

"Oh! Werner doesn't get many visitors. Only that nice man next door. Stan?" She flipped through the admittance book, but Nate was focused on the gap between her front teeth.

"Yeah, I know Stan," Nate said, his voice harsher than he'd intended. He wasn't particularly angry with Stan. After all, Stan was just drinking coffee when Brooke started throwing herself at him. He didn't even look particularly interested, so it wasn't exactly anger Nate was feeling. Jealousy. Envy. The urge to smash in those perfect teeth. But not anger.

The nurse buzzed the door open, and Nate walked out of the desert heat into the cool climate controlled interior of the convalescent home. It smelled of antiseptic, the walls yellowed with age, and chipped linoleum tiles on the floor were well worn but spotless. A vase filled with dried desert flowers, layer of dust coating them, sat atop the nurses' station. Nate walked down the short hallway.

He stood in the doorway, watching Werner sleep. He hadn't seen his father in years. His father had always been old, it seemed. Too old for his mother in many ways. This was different. Laying in that hospital bed, it seemed like he'd aged far too many years. His skin was pale and his eyes sunken. He was skinny, seemed frail. His face looked thin and weak, and his jawline was changed as it looked like he'd lost all of his teeth. He was nothing like the man Nate had last seen twenty years ago. It was still his father, though. Same scar running from the corner of his eye to his jawline. Same as Nate's.

"You can talk to him. He might not understand, but it helps. Some days are better than others, and he's mostly confused. On bad days he won't speak at all, except maybe a few disjointed words here and there." She paused for a moment, looking at Nate uncomfortably. "I'm so sorry." The nurse tried to smile a sympathetic smile, but Nate was distracted by the look in her eyes that she got from seeing all of her patients eventually die.

"I know," Nate said. He'd been putting this off. He could've come that first afternoon while Brooke was getting settled in at the house. Or the next, after his day at the Real World Monitor. But he didn't. He wasn't even planning on coming today, but it just seemed like the best way to get out of the house and cool down before going into work at the paper.

Now, standing there, it was hard to feel distant. It was hard to remember all the times that his father had disapproved of him. All the times his father pushed him into sports teams, only to stay on the base during the games at which Nate would fail miserably. All the times Nate would show him his report card, all marks in the eighties or nineties, only to have him go off about how the only real way to learn what the world was like was to work and suffer, join the army and become a man. All the times Werner called him a pansy, like when he cried after gashing his face open on the rebar in the street, the wound that gave him that scar down his face. Nate remembered it, sure, but he felt separated from it now, looking at the frail old man confined to the bed.

"Dad... it's me. It's Nate."

Werner looked up, his eyes glassy.

"Do you understand me?"

"Irving?" Werner said, his lips dry and cracked.

"No, Dad. I'm not Uncle Irving. I'm Nate." Irving was Werner's older brother. Irving had also been in the military, but retired early and became a welder. He died of a heart attack. Nate was still pretty young at the time, and they drove all the way to Florida to go to the funeral. Werner never cried.

"Have you gone AWOL again? Irving, those dancing girls aren't worth it. You get caught again they'll throw you in the brig."

"No Dad. It's Nate."

Werner laid back down and smacked his lips. Nate spied the glass of water on the bedside table, paper bendy straw already bent. He picked it up and brought it to Werner's lips. Werner sipped, coughed, and sipped some more.

"I know you don't know what's going on, Dad, but I screwed up. I screwed everything up. People just expected too much from me. I lied." Nate stopped and breathed in deeply. He'd admitted it before, but it felt different this time. Maybe because it was to his father. "I got caught, and now I've lost everything. No credible paper will hire me, my wife hates me, and the only reason I still have a home is because you're here." Nate dropped his head, holding his father's soft hand. Tears started rolling down his face, slow at first, but soon Nate started gulping in breaths.

"What do you want?" Werner asked, a scowl crossing his scarred face.

The question caught Nate off guard. He felt ten years old again. Unsympathetic father, emotional son.

"Nothing Dad. I don't want anything."

"Then what are you doing here?"

Nate stood up, rubbed the tears from his eyes and sucked in a quick breath. "I don't know, Dad. Some kind of closure. Some kind of acceptance. I guess it doesn't work that way."

"Why don't you leave?"

"Yeah." Nate turned to leave. Even after the stroke, his father was still a cantankerous old bastard. "Wait. The truck. Dad, do you know where the keys are?"

"Key?" Werner said, his eyebrows raising and his eyes wide. "Irving! You know about the key? Oh, thank God. They've locked me here, and I didn't know what would become of things."

Nate stood in the doorway, looking back. His father suddenly seemed so animated. He was sitting up, gesturing wildly with his hands. His irises seemed blackened out by his pupils, dwarfed by the whites of his eyes.

"They all wanted it, you know! They all wanted it, but I knew what it was. I had to lock it up safe! I had to keep the key close to me." Werner looked around suspiciously, before turning over in his bed and reaching beneath the mattress and the bedspring. His hands moved swiftly and deftly, searching until he found a small key, dirty string looped around it like it was meant to go around a child's neck so they could get into the house for lunch.

"Here it is. Take it."

Nate walked over and held out his hand. Werner pressed it into his hand. "I got it in the Sahara. Irving, you keep it safe." Nate looked down at the key in his hand. It was a small and brass, looking more like a locker key than a key for a rusty old pickup. Nate looked back at his father, who was still staring at him, slack jawed. It was almost a look of terror, if Nate believed his father was even capable of that level of emotion. "Put it on! Keep it safe!" Werner urged.

Werner had been to the Sahara. It was back during the Iraq war. He was in a small military plane, four of them including the pilot. The plane lost all power and crashed into the desert. Everyone died upon impact, except Werner. Maybe it was from his years living in Red Valley, or maybe he was just too crotchety to quit, but he started walking. Three days later, or so his story went, he ran into a man that gave him water and took him to Telagh. Werner never talked about it much, once referred to him as a one-armed Jew, but otherwise didn't give many details.

Nate was certain it had happened just as Werner had told him. Werner was not the sort of man who would make up stories. But turning the key over and over in his hand, Nate couldn't believe that Werner found it in the desert. Stamped on one side of the key were the words Made In The USA. The idea that Werner had gotten this in the Sahara seemed completely implausible.

"Don't let them take it, Irving. Don't let them find it."

"I won't, Dad." Nate pulled the string over his head, slipped the key under his shirt and patted it. He smiled at the old man, patronizing him.

"Why do they stand looking at the sky? The day has come when he will judge the world with justice by the man he has appointed. He has given proof of this to everyone." Werner was waving his arms around, gesturing more and more erratically. His eyes grew wider, spittle dripping from his mouth. "We eagerly await a Saviour by the power that enables him to bring everything under his control. He will transform our lowly bodies so that they will be like his glorious body!"

Before Nate could stop him, his father was on his feet. The sheets fell to the floor, and Werner stood there, pale sickly skin stretched over his protruding bones, wearing only his stained jockeys as he raised his emaciated arms up in the air.

"Dad! Calm down! Get back in bed!"

"Repent! Repent now or be cast down into the lake of boiling blood!"

Suddenly the nurses were at the door, pulling on Nate's shoulders to get him out of the room. "What did you say to him?" one of them asked, but Nate couldn't respond. He just looked at his father, a man of control, of discipline, screaming like a madman before being physically pulled back into his bed, arms strapped into restraints.

"The Lord is coming! Don't grumble against each other, brothers, or you will be judged. The Judge is standing at the door!"

13

Snow. Snow slowly drifted down out of the blackness of the moonless sky on the mountain retreat. It'd been years since the man inside had a name. Around these parts, he was known only as Umba. He sat at his Olivetti manual typewriter tapping on the keys, the hammers striking a ribbon used so many times it barely made the shadow of a letter on the page. Didn't matter, though, because Umba knew no one would read it. He did it to keep his mind keen. He did it so that the life he once had was not lost.

> My Dearest. It's been too long since I've written. I know I've told you this a thousand times, but I need to be sure you understand. I've moved on.

The retreat was a small log cabin, handmade by Umba himself, before his beard grew long and grey, before his hands grew weak with age. Each log harvested from the surrounding forests, fit together without nails. One axe, aching muscles.

Clack clack, the hammers hit the paper in quick succession.

He'd lost track of how much time had passed since building it. He could tell by his grey hair and missing teeth that it had been many, many years.

> But sometimes I feel like you're the only one I can talk to, even though you'll never read these words. I can't talk to my wife about these things. She doesn't understand.

The wind picked up, blowing the snow in through the cracks in the walls. The fire pit in the middle of the room burned warmly, but nothing was sufficient to ward off the cold on an evening like this one. At the altitude Umba lived at, it snowed year round, and the only thing that broke the blisteringly cold winds were the coniferous trees. He didn't dare go above the tree line on the mountainside. He needed the protection of the forests, not only from the cold, but from people, and whatever else was out there.

> I've been having... feelings... like something is going to happen. You know how it was when we were together? Like we had some sort of... I don't know... psychic bond or something? That's silly, I know. Nothing like that really exists, but I can't deny that I feel something. Something pulling me somewhere. It's like a craving.

Clack clack clack.

Umba was engulfed in his writing. He'd often come into the cabin for warmth, and time to think. He was part of the community up here, but he was always the different one. He was the outsider, so to collect himself together he'd find quiet time, once, maybe twice a week, and just type. The images and words in his head would become so vivid that he'd neglect everything happening in the world around him. That's probably why he didn't hear the rough cabin door slowly creaking open.

```
Could you be coming back? Could it be true?
No... no, I can't allow myself to think
that. I've got a life here. I'm married.
It's too late for us.
```

He didn't notice the hand, black, calloused, pushing the door open with a stealthiness that one wouldn't expect from something that cast the seven-foot tall silhouette.

Clack clack.

```
But I have to know why you left. I need to
know if you're all right.
```

The light of the small fire in the middle of the room illuminated the immense creature. Huge, hulking, with a mildew and skunk spray stench lingering around it. Hands, almost human, tense and at the ready. Covered with long, reddish-brown fur, one couldn't make out the creature's exact shape, but what was unmistakable was the pure strength, the violence this creature was capable of.

```
You're right. I should tell my wife. Be
honest. I'm not cheating on her, not loving
her any less. I'm getting closure on
something that happened a long time ago.
That's all.
```

The creature was directly behind Umba now. His face looking down at the typewriter, fingers tapping away on the keys, the loud clicks of the hammers on the paper. The creature, dwarfing him in its presence, raised up its massive limbs.

```
I will. I will do it. It may all come to
nothing, but I'll trust that voice inside of
me.
```

"AAARRROOOUUUUUU!!!" howled the creature, deafeningly loud in the tiny cabin. The man turned to see the massive ape-like creature in front of him, his eyes wide in terror, mouth agape, jolting violently from the abject terror of the beast.

"Holy shit!" Umba yelled, hand quickly reaching up to his heart. "Cinnamon! Holy fuck, don't do that to me! My ticker can't handle it!"

The Bigfoot leaned down, laughing in her grunting, throaty voice. "Uh uh uh uh uh!" She went down on her knees, as to look Umba in the eyes. "Umba," she said, eyes tearing up from laughter.

"Yeah yeah yeah, you got me that time," Umba said, fear gone, and the humour of the situation hitting him. "Oh, sweetheart, you're terrible." He leaned in and gave Cinnamon a quick kiss on her dark black lips, and looked into her eyes. "It's so unfair, because you know I can't stay mad at you."

Cinnamon looked deep into his eyes. "Umba?"

"You can tell, can't you?" he said. "Yeah, I need to do something."

He'd been a drifter for years. He'd ridden the rails, traveled all across the continent, jumping borders and occasionally running from the police, until he'd found his mountain retreat. It had only been a few weeks until he'd met her. He'd been scavenging for food, living out of a lean-to at the time, as he didn't know how long he'd stay. He certainly didn't know the mountainside would become his home. Then, he'd spotted her. She had been walking down by the river. She was younger then, too. He was instantly curious by this unbelievable creature of the forests. He'd called out to her, but she'd known to run from the hairless ones. He'd been left on the mountainside, looking down at where she was, her massive footprints still visible in the mud on the riverbank.

It'd taken weeks before he spotted her again. She'd run, but he had been patient. He'd learned that much. Of course, at that time he couldn't even conceive of falling in love with this beast, this creature of the forests, but every time he found her, Cinnamon allowed him a bit closer until they finally touched hands. They both had realized it. They were meant to be together.

"I need to go back to my home town. I need to finish my business there," he said, the wind picking up again and blowing a frigid breeze through the sparse cabin walls.

"Uh uh.. Guh…" she said back. Her features turning from laughter into a look of concern, not only for what was happening in the cabin but for her husband's emotional welfare in general.

"Yes, it's about her. I need to know what happened to her. Why she left. It changed my life, changed who I am, and I never found out why. Something has changed, and... and I can't put my finger on it. It's time for me to finally answer all those questions that have been following me all these years."

Umba got to his feet, held out his hand, and Cinnamon took it, helping herself up. She wasn't a young Bigfoot anymore. Umba took a moment to wrap himself up in the wolf-fur coat he'd made himself, and they left the cramped confines of the cabin.

"Garrrhuh... muh uh..." Cinnamon said in her native tongue. After years together, they'd learned how to communicate. She understood English, and he understood Bigfoot, although the complexities, the subtleties of speaking each others languages, was still too difficult even after these decades together. They spoke their own languages, Cinnamon speaking Bigfoot and Umba responding in English. Umba even had to come up with Cinnamon's name, while she approximated his own.

"That's why I love you, honey. I know. You always think of what's best for me. You're such a good wife," Umba said, looking sideways at her. He could see the concern on her face. He'd never asked to return to the lands of the humans before, even when times were difficult and food was scarce. Adjusting to the life of the forests was extraordinarily difficult, and there were times that Umba barely survived. She knew that the humans had machines to make their lives easier, strange metal animals they drove around in, plentiful food that came in thin plastic peels.

"Should we tell the others?" Umba asked, looking into Cinnamon's dark eyes.

Cinnamon and Umba turned and looked up at the clearing in front of them. The small village of forty, maybe fifty Bigfoot beneath the rocky overhang of the mountainside, protecting them from the winds and light snow. Some families huddled closely together, protecting their young, while others stood guard, patrolling through the surrounding forests.

This was their home. This was their community, and now Umba planned on leaving.

14

"Once you weed out the really awful stuff, it's not so bad," Nate said, trying to make the best of things as he lay in bed, flipping through back issues of the Real World Monitor. The day hadn't gone well. Another day at the paper, extrapolating upon people's outright lies from the bizarre stories in the letter pile, and then home to Brooke, who had silently delivered dinner onto a plate. After dishes and unpacking a few more boxes, they'd retired to bed, and Brooke spent the evening online, scrolling through celebrity gossip sites and online tabloids. At least the internet had gotten hooked up. "There's a lot of racist stuff people mail in, or stuff like the Jews were behind the 9/11 attack. I hate that shit. At least if it's Lizard People behind the attack, I can get behind it. It's a lie, obviously, but it's not like it's singling anyone out."

"Yeah," Brooke said, noncommittally. She swiped across a few screens on her iPad, reading articles about celebrities. Housewives and douchebags on the beach, people who never did anything worth being recognized for, yet getting celebrity status anyway. To Brooke, though, they deserved celebrity just for being who they were. Maybe it was just a cheap lowbrow form of escapism, but after the day Brooke had gone through, it was exactly what she needed.

"I've never really been politically active, you know? It's always just reporting. You look, you see something, you write it down. The moment I try to get involved, like, try to change something, it all turns to shit. I was a reporter. I should just report, right? No, I have to open my big mouth, try to make a point, try to right a wrong…"

"And look where the fuck we are."

"I know. I know I got us here."

"I don't understand you. You know that? It's like I'm living with a stranger. I don't even know who you are anymore."

"Yeah, it feels that way."

"You're all hot and heavy to get me to love this dump of a town… if you can even call it a town… more like a collection of weirdoes stuck in the left armpit of the world… you want me to like it here, and then the second, the very second I start talking to someone, you start having a spaz. Is your ego really that delicate? Do you really have that little self-esteem?"

"Now wait! You know what you were doing!"

"I'm going to sleep," Brooke said abruptly, rolling over and dropping her iPad onto the floor indelicately. With one swift flick of her hand she turned off the bedside light, leaving Nate sitting, steaming, beside her. No chance for retaliation, just a conversation to ensure he wouldn't sleep well. The anger stuck in his throat like a fishbone.

Scratch scratch scratch.

Yip yip yip yip yip!

"Toodles!" Brooke yelled, her own frustration welling up into a voice that was much louder and more aggressive than was warranted. "Shut the fuck up!"

Of course, Toodles continued yipping, as if Brooke's burst of anger was simply her joining in on the barking.

"Fuck's sake, Nate. Fix this shit!"

Nate dragged himself out of bed. The long day wore on him, but there was still more to do. Without a word to quiet the yapping dog he pulled on an undershirt and pyjama pants while actively avoiding looking at his wife. Earlier in the day he'd rummaged through a dozen boxes while Brooke organized dinner, finding the flashlight so as to not repeat the night before. He opened the bedroom door, and along with Toodles, he walked gingerly down the stairs to the main floor. He turned on the kitchen lights, walked through the laundry room and out the back door. His mind harkened back to his childhood, sneaking down the stairs in the darkness to watch monster movies on television. Werewolves and alien blobs, skeletons reaching out with bony hands.

The moment he opened that back door, he regretted it. Toodles, yipping like she'd had espresso in her water dish, raced through the door and out into the darkness of the desert night.

"Shit!" Nate said, teeth clenched. This was, seriously, the last thing he needed. "Toodles, get back here! Now!" He took a few steps out into the desert night, flashlight shining into the blackness. The cool air hit him, bare legs and a t-shirt, as he breathed in deeply. Even in the dryness of the desert, the night air smelled slightly damp. He breathed in deeper, but there was something else in the night, a smell of fur, a hot, wet animal smell, acrid and pungent. He darted the anemic beam his flashlight around, side to side, trying to catch a glance of the furiously yipping dog.

Eyes. Reflecting in the darkness. Red. Two pairs. Three, maybe.

Nate's stomach dropped. He quickly went through possibilities in his head, wondering if they could be coyotes, maybe dogs, abandoned and gone feral. They were large, he could tell, but from just the red eyes, reflecting the porch light, it was impossible to tell what the hell they were. Then, the worst sound he could imagine.

Click.

The door of the crooked house had slowly swung closed, latch on the inside clicking into place, locking him outside in the darkness, the glowing eyes out there, watching him.

Yip yip yip yip yip!

Nate raced back to the door and yanked on the handle with no luck. Then he banged his fists on the door. "Brooke! Open the door!" he yelled, his voice growing more frantic with each second that passed. "Fuck!"

Yip yip yip yip yip… crunch.

Then a grisly sound came from the desert. Tearing flesh, sucking, chewing. The *'schlop schlop'* sound chilling him. Nate turned his back to the door, flashlight still searching the darkness, trying to discern what it could be out there.

Then silence.

His light darted around, and finally caught the head of something. Human, he assumed, but even in the jolting light of the flashlight shaking in his hand, he could discern short grey fur covered its bony facial structure. Its eyes, completely red, were wide apart on its head, and two long teeth protruded from its long face. It had rags across its shoulders as if someone had attempted to dress it, but its razor sharp claws, yellow and splintered, had torn them apart. It sprinted at him on all fours, mouth wide, teeth bared.

Nate panicked. He leapt off of the rickety back porch and raced around the corner of the house, aiming for the front door.

"Scree scree scree!" screeched the rat-like creature as it closed the distance between them with ease. One clawed hand swiped, reaching for him, and the razor sharp claws scraped down the back of Nate's calf, splitting open the skin and digging deep into the soft flesh. Blood gushed out, and pain shot through him. He tumbled to the ground, and instantly, in a flurry of clawed hands and feet, the thing was on top of him. It wasn't heavy, and wasn't as big as a man. More like a ten-year-old, but swift and deadly, reeking of wet fur and the unmistakable coppery smell of blood.

Nate kicked instinctively. He'd never had any training in fighting at all, but somehow he'd mustered it, bringing his knee up and planting his foot into the belly of the rat creature, kicking it off of him. It tumbled backwards, and Nate was up, running, limping, trying to get to the front of the house.

Thump!

Nate tumbled, slammed in the gut. At first, he thought it was another one of those things, but no. He'd run into the sofa, still discarded in the front yard. He scrambled through the piles of discarded furniture, pictures Brooke had thrown away, and everything familiar from his childhood.

He felt something sharp dig itself deep into his hand. Darts. He'd fallen on his dartboard. Quickly he pulled a couple plastic-sheathed darts from the board. He could hear the footfalls of creatures around him, but holding a sofa cushion as a shield, he stood up, unsteadily on his wounded leg.

The flashlight, dropped on the ground when he'd fallen, caught the feet of one of his attackers. He threw the darts wildly! He heard a 'thunk' sound, and the creature screeched, retreating momentarily.

He scrabbled around quickly, grabbing anything else he could use as a weapon, something to defend himself. Pulling up what he thought was another cushion, he realized it was his childhood plush animal.

"You threw out Iggy? You bitch!" Nate cursed, throwing Iggy to the side and continuing running his hands over his discarded possessions.

He managed to pick a green steel coat rack Werner had brought home from the base. Nate was no longer thinking straight. His mind was no longer on the future, on the troubles of his life. He was thinking of the next minute, and nothing else.

Something leapt at him. He pointed the coat rack out in front of him like a spear, bracing himself, as the creature bashed into him. He held it at arm's length, and the rat-thing, this one smaller than the other, clawed at him but didn't have the reach to get to him. It gnashed its teeth trying to get at his hands and arms, but Nate kept him far away. Rat kids. That's what they were. Just kids, or so it seemed, but half rat. He might have had some sympathy if not for the ferocity of the attack.

His mind on the immediate threat, he'd left his back open, and another rat kid leapt on him, raking its jagged claws across his face, digging into him as the blood sprayed across the old furniture and the dry desert floor. The coat rack fell from his hands as the agony hit Nate.

"Gaah!" he screamed, reaching up and bending over, throwing the one rat kid into another, both tumbling onto the packed earth.

Nate turned and ran, forgetting about the front door of the house and racing for the old brown pickup truck. His eyes were wild as he grappled with the handle of the vehicle, but it, too, was locked. He crouched, as if to hide behind the corner of the truck. He squinted his eyes, and as the creature rounded the corner, Nate grabbed it and slammed it to the ground.

He pummelled down on it with his fists, like a schoolyard bully on an unsuspecting kid, but the creature still clawed up at his forearms with those deadly claws, scratching long red rivers of torn flesh all along them.

Tumbling. The third of the rat kids, the largest, bowled into him and they tumbled into some desert brush. Nate, bleeding from both arms, his face, and the long, terrible wounds down his calf, lay prone. The creature, sensing his inability to defend himself, reared up, hands wide, claws ready for the kill.

"Scree scree scree!" the other two rat kids screeched, flanking him on both sides.

There's a moment that every wild animal must feel when they realize it's over. The lion has the gazelle by the throat, the owl flies off with the rabbit, when the prey knows that there's no more fight to be had. Nate looked up, hoping for sympathy. Hoping for humanity, but finding none.

Bang!

The darkness of the night was suddenly pierced by the flash of the gun barrel, the sudden explosion of sound ringing in Nate's ears. The rat kid slumped down upon him, hot blood gushing over his face from the hole dead centre through the rat kid's face.

"Scree scree scree!" the other two rat kids screeched, racing off into the darkness of the desert night. Nate exhaled, just laying there with the dead creature atop him. Pain shot through his face, his body, but he'd had his reprieve.

Nate looked up. He saw a man walk over and pick up the fallen flashlight. He returned and shined the light on his face.

Not a face. A bloody pulp of a face. Muscles and bone exposed, no skin, just raw flesh and cartilage. His white dress shirt stained red all down the collar, tan trench coat splattered with blood. His eyes were the worst. Wide and gaping, only the slightest pieces of mangled flesh remained for eyelids. His teeth bare, lipless, and entirely visible cheekbone and chin, ripped flesh all along his hairline. He looked down at Nate.

"Looks like you need more help than I do," Edgar hissed in his throaty, rough voice.

Suddenly the porch light came on, flooding the front yard with light, exposing the torn furniture, the sprays of blood, and Nate, prone on his back, struggling to push the corpse of the rat kid off of him. Brooke burst through the doorway, panicked. "I heard the screaming and the banging!" she yelled. "Was that a gunshot?"

Edgar turned, bloody-faced, and, with his horrible, piercing eyes, looked at Brooke.

"Oh... oh god... please," Brooke suddenly pleaded, looking down at the gun, still smoking, in Edgar's hand.

"Don't worry about me," Edgar gurgled, "your man here is losing blood. You got a car?"

Nate looked up. Arms burning, face too. He was losing blood. It was all over him, soaking his t-shirt, coating his legs and arms.

"Yeah... I got a car," she said, throwing him the house keys from her hand, "please... please don't hurt me..." Her eyes danced back and forth between Edgar's face, his gun, and the inhuman body lying bloody on the ground.

Edgar caught the keys, looked at them momentarily, and threw them back at her. "You drive," he said, "Dr. Bhijani is out of town. Nearest hospital is in Pronghorn Mesa. He'll last that long." He reached down and pulled Nate to his feet, wrapping Nate's arm around his shoulder for support.

"What the fuck was that thing?" Nate asked, growing incoherent, looking at the body of the rat kid on the ground.

"Lots of weird shit in the desert," Edgar said, "no one ever tell you that?"

Brooke thrust herself under Nate's other arm, and they dragged him to the red Miata. They dropped him in the back seat, laying down, and Edgar buckled himself into the passenger seat. "Who are you?" she asked.

Edgar reached into his pocket and pulled out a card. "Edgar Catafalque. Obscurologist, Parapsychologist, and Conspiracy Investigator," he said, "but don't tell anyone." At that point, he might have smiled, but without a face, it was lost.

The car peeled down the dusty roads, deep into the desert night. Brooke, not the most comfortable driver, had her eyes focused on the road ahead, white knuckles and pedal to the floor. And as the Miata traveled further and further away from the town of Red Valley, they didn't notice the light in the sky, a small ring, growing moment by moment above the empty desert. They drove on, passing beyond the rocky ridges and boulders, off to Pronghorn Mesa, and far, far behind them, the light grew closer and closer to the ground, hovering, saucer-like, above the desert floor, until a beam of green light shone down, blindingly, to the red earth below it.

Moments later, the light flickered off, and, still illuminated by the ring of light, the naked girl stood motionless as the saucer flew off, leaving her alone in the darkness.

15

Days passed under the sweltering sun, the chilled nights, and the boredom of looking out over the same blank landscape, the endless horizon in all directions. And the voices.

Phaedra felt the intoxication of passing time. Maybe it was the dry desert air, the zen-like empty scenery, or maybe it was the shack. The shack. Nothing more than a pile of ramshackle boards and nails, the power cord from the batteries and the solar panels, and the chained door. During the long desert nights, Phaedra would lay awake, looking at the patterns of light projected onto the tent walls, the light that was slipping out through the gaps in the shack's walls. Bright enough to overcome the dull glow of Phaedra's own luminescent skeleton, shimmering beneath her flesh and organs.

The ghostly skeleton glowed faintly throughout the nights. When she relaxed, it was dim, but she knew that in times of stress it somehow glowed increasingly brightly. Still, even at its dullest glow, it made it difficult to sleep. The glow came from within, so closing her eyelids did very little to rest her eyes.

"Help us…" whispered the wind. Almost imperceptibly. Maybe Phaedra hadn't heard it at all. Desert plays tricks with your mind.

And the days passed. Three, four, five. They'd said they'd be back in a week, but Phaedra knew how the military dealt with weird little anomalies. They'd ignore them as best they could, send them to mysterious subunits within subunits. Phaedra had been tasked to deal with anomalies before. She'd had to deal with the cockroaches, and was then told never to tell anyone about it ever again.

It had been the big meltdown in Indiana. The one that they covered up so well that no one ever heard of it. Never made the history books, the news, not even the local chit-chat. Cockroaches had gotten into the reaction chamber. Anything within that reaction chamber is, with nearly a hundred percent accuracy, going to die. Fast. Radiation has this nasty way of breaking DNA chains, unravelling them like a malicious cat with a ball of yarn. You are the yarn. Once your DNA is altered, even a little, cancer is often the result.

"We're damned… each of us…" Phaedra swore she heard on the desert wind.

Nearly one hundred percent. Not always. The 'how and why' of the incident didn't matter, especially to Phaedra, who'd been part of the cleanup. They told her that the suit of protective gear would protect her from the radiation, that the protocols were all in place to ensure they were all shielded. They had top-secret Saturnium radiation sinkholes in place, which, of course, the military has had for years. Why didn't they bring them to Chernobyl? The nuclear meltdown there was obviously a distraction for something much more sinister.

Phaedra was sopping up the glowing nuclear runoff with the grapheme oxide equivalent of a mop, laced with a mineral known only as 27-4. Then they appeared. Glowing cockroaches. Impossible, but there they were. No bigger than a regular old German cockroach you might find under the fridge, not shooting lasers from their eyes or vomiting acid. Just glowing. Phaedra had told her C.O. and soon there were dozens of nameless high-ranking officials on site. They'd left with the cockroaches in jars, and that was the last of it.

Then her skeleton started glowing. Phaedra wondered if the protective gear had simply failed, or if it was tampered with, like a weird experiment the military was running. Wouldn't be the first time the military complex had used unwitting soldiers as laboratory rats. She wondered what happened to the other soldiers at the clean-up, but she knew better than to ask.

After that, the military started giving her more assignments where she was placed on her own. Remote spots. The desert was just one stop in a number of stops. Chocolate Mountain, Dulce Base, Club 33.

By the fifth day, sixth maybe, as time was getting difficult to track, the voices became more pronounced, and Phaedra was hearing them here and there, welling up on the wind, then dying down. And the shack was just another frustration. It just sat there, decrepit-looking and nondescript, hiding something important. Important enough for the military to post a soldier in the middle of a desert. It nagged at Phaedra, irritating her like a sore tooth, one that she tried to distract herself from, but was unable to keep her mind from going back to. Curiosity bit at her whenever she saw the shack, the faded wood and rusted nails, light glowing from the cracks.

"Torment…" the voice said, much more clearly. Phaedra sat up from the spot she'd set out in the shadow of the tent. She had seen that ghostly mist growing above the shack on the second day, maybe third, but she attributed that to stress, mental breakdown, possibly a bad meal. She thought it possible that the water had been drugged, but the lack of further hallucinations had ended that suspicion.

She got up, grabbed her M16 and walked the perimeter. Nothing. Not even a desert lizard. Not a sparrow. Nothing. She walked further and further out into the desert until the shack was sitting on the horizon, but still, found nothing. The desert was empty. No one was needing help.

"Lost... we are all lost..." the voices spoke, "...my love..."

As time wore on, they became more discernible. Sometimes still a murmur, or strange chants, screams, cries of agony. Yet other times undeniably clear, voices begging for mercy, for leniency, for relief.

"Send a message..." one of the disembodied voices spoke. She looked at the shack. She wondered if the voices were coming from the shack. Was it the entrance to an underground city? A subterranean prison? Why would they put a lone soldier to guard it? Why was she guarding nothing but a shack in the middle of the desert?

"Fuck off!" Phaedra responded, sitting at the fire. She heated her rations and was trying to eat. After the curiosity she had about the voices wore off, they became an annoyance. The world was weird, and Phaedra had firsthand knowledge of that, but voices in the wind were nothing compared to half of what she'd seen, glowing cockroaches notwithstanding.

"How could I have been so blind..."

"Where is my love... my heart aches..."

Phaedra plugged her ears, trying to keep the voices out, but it didn't help. She couldn't tell if they were actually voices, or just in her head, and it didn't matter. She just wanted them to stop.

And far off in the desert, looking towards the small shack on the horizon, a creature looked up from its seemingly endless search for food. Doglike, but the size of a bear, hairless, lips peeled back up to expose its sharp, ragged teeth, and a row of spines jutting from its back. It sniffed the ground, and the rest of the pack loped by, snarling and nipping at one another. It picked up its head, took another long look at the shack before loping off with its pack into the unending desolation of the desert.

16

"Rat-Kids attack Red Valley! Fantastic!" Mr. Leone bellowed out loud enough for all the other reporters to hear as well, make them jealous of the new guy. "Front page! Good job, Scarface!"

"Yeah, thanks, Mr. Leone," Nate said. The 'Scarface' name irritated him like a splinter, but it looked like it was going to stick around the office. It didn't help when Nate returned to work after his three days in the hospital, stitches across his face, walking with a crutch.

After they'd arrived at the hospital that night, they'd rushed both Nate and Edgar into the emergency ward. Nate had lost blood, but somehow the claws of the strange little rat children had missed slicing through any vital arteries or into any organs. The worst he had was the long slice down the back of his leg, and they'd stitched that up, pumped him full of antibiotics and painkillers, and gave him a bed for the night.

"Why… why did they have to kill her?" Brooke wept at the side of his bed. She'd been strong the entire ride to the hospital and helped him through the agonizing moments before they could administer anything to help him with the pain, but once he was safe, Brooke wept. Nate was safe, but Toodles was gone.

Nate didn't cry. It seemed uncharacteristic of him, as he liked dogs, but there was a side of him that thought it was natural selection. If she had been stupid enough to race out into the darkness, those creatures out there, then she deserved what she'd gotten. Following that thought was a feeling of shame. It was a terrible way to die, and Toodles, for all her faults, was a loveable little thing.

Nate had never had a pet of his own. They'd never owned a dog or a cat or anything within the confines of his childhood house. His father didn't think animals belonged in the house. He said that the fur was hard on the washing machine, but that was ridiculous as he never did his own laundry. Nate ached for a pet in that house, a friend in a friendless town, someone he could confide in, someone to share his experience with. Instead, he had no one. Once he moved to Los Angeles, his mother felt that keeping an animal in a tiny apartment wasn't humane. The closest he'd ever come to actually owning a pet was Brooke's cat, all scraggly and mischievous, and then after it ran off, Toodles. But she was never his pet. She was Brooke's. He'd liked it when the cat would curl up on his lap as he sat at his keyboard writing articles late into the night, push pens off the edge of the desk and onto the floor, but Toodles was never his dog. She didn't listen to Nate, didn't come when he called.

Toodles barely tolerated him, but as Brooke wept he couldn't keep from tearing up as well.

Edgar was rushed into the emergency ward as well, protesting the entire way. The registration nurse threw up as soon as he walked in.

"Get that guy on a gurney!" yelled an orderly, clearly out of his depth. A nurse nearly bowled Edgar over with the gurney and suddenly three other orderlies were surrounding them. Edgar was snatched off his feet and found himself wondering how they'd gotten him on his back so quickly.

"Strap him down!" the initial orderly yelled. "This guy is a crack head from the city!"

"What do you mean?" another orderly yelled, a young man with glasses and male-pattern baldness. "How do you know he's on crack?" He spoke quickly, hands moving swiftly on the straps and buckles, fastening them more rapidly than Edgar could think to resist.

"I read about it on the internet! There was a guy who took crack and he cut his own face off and fed it to his dog!"

"No way!" Male-Pattern-Baldness orderly said, suddenly impressed with Edgar, who was still looking around, flustered.

"Sir," the nurse yelled into his face. She seemed to think that if she spoke loudly enough a drug addict would become coherent. "Sir, where is the dog?"

"The dog?" Edgar said, looking from side to side. "The Rat-Kids ate the dog!"

"What was that?" a third orderly chimed in. "He thinks rats ate his face?"

"No!" the nurse yelled overtop of them all. "He fed his dog to the rats!"

"What the hell is everyone talking about!?!" Edgar yelled vociferously as they hustled him down the hall and away from Nate and Brooke. The next day, Nate was released, telling them that he'd been mugged rather than corroborate Edgar's story. Edgar was kept for further examination.

Nate spent the following two days recovering in bed. He'd pulled his laptop onto a vintage Florentine serving tray and kept it on his lap to type out the story of the rat kids. It was only one story, far from his quota, but the drugs made him foggy. Still, he craved that fogginess once they wore off and he felt the throbbing pain from his leg.

"It's true," Nate said to Mr. Leone. He had the scratches across his face to prove it. Scarface. One side had his childhood scar, the other, new ones in the making.

"Ha ha!" Mr. Leone laughed his deep belly laugh. "You hear that, Hardy! It's true!"

"Har har har," Hardy joined in.

"Hey!" Mike Rant, pinch-faced and flush, yelled over his desk. "I'm trying to write here!"

"Of course it's true," Mr. Leone said, patting Nate roughly on the back, "we print news here. It's all true!"

"Yeah," Nate said, bitterness in his voice palpable to anyone who was paying the tiniest bit of attention to him, "well, I've got a check-up at the hospital today, so I'll need to take off early. Do you have anything for me?"

"Matter of fact, I do. Werner was stationed outside of town, right? I need someone to check it out. Your dad ever take you out there?"

"Uh… no… but… they won't let me do that…" Nate said. The base closed down decades ago, took most of the businesses in town with it. Nate thought they would at least keep a skeleton crew at bases like that, probably for insurance reasons more than anything. They make sure no one comes on the base, make sure the place doesn't burn down. Nate couldn't just walk up to it and start poking around. For that matter, what was out there that needed to be looked into?

"You've been gone a while, I'll give you that. There isn't anyone out there. Not for a long time. Military pulled out and that was that. Always had an ugly feel about the place. Only ones that go out there are local teens looking for a place to drink, drag race on the streets, that kind of thing. Still, there've been sightings."

"Sightings?"

"Chupacabra."

Chupacabra. The word stuck in Nate's head the entire drive out to the hospital. Two months ago he was in line to be the head writer at a nationwide news program, with promises of air time, maybe even anchor, and now he was going to write about a chupacabra. This is what it had come to. Nate wasn't even mad. He accepted it. He had to. This was his life now.

The drive back to Pronghorn Mesa was growing increasingly dull. The desert was barren, lacking landmarks, and Nate found himself drifting off, thinking about the Rat Kids. They were rat-like, for sure, but now with the benefit of time and perspective, he questioned himself. Maybe it was just some sort of cougar, maybe a small family of them, mangy, hairless cougars. While implausible, it was far more likely than some sort of rat-human hybrid.

"Looks like the antibiotics are working," the Doctor said. His name was Dr. Eugene Creakie, and he looked more like a mad scientist than a doctor. White haired, thick glasses, unshaven. "We'll keep you on them for another couple weeks. Really make sure that you don't get anything. That leg will heal up nicely. It wasn't as bad as it looked. You might get a nasty scar though. Did my best to clean it up, but he really got you good." He looked up at Nate's face. "Other ones probably won't be so noticeable. Not as prominent as the one you already have."

"How is the man who brought me in?" Nate questioned. "Edgar."

"Edgar? Oh... yes... I can't really comment on the... uh... condition of other patients, but I might be able to allow you to talk to him. His injuries are... uh... quite horrific..."

"I remember." Nate stood up, leaving the crutch behind. He still limped, but it was nowhere as painful as it had been a few days prior, and his strength had mostly returned. "Thank you, Dr. Creakie."

Dr. Creakie left him sitting in the waiting room for a half hour until he was confident that he could allow Edgar a visitor. Three days, and no change in his mental state. He was beginning to think that it wasn't meth, but an undiagnosed mental illness, and the hospital wasn't set up for something this extreme. He'd have to go to a city for that.

"Now, steel yourself," he said to Nate, "maybe in the heat of the moment you were more concerned with your mugging, but now that you're calm, this might be... disturbing."

"Thank you, doctor."

"Brace yourself. It ain't pretty." Dr. Creakie opened the door and allowed Nate into the room.

Edgar was fully strapped into a bed. Arms bound with thick white padded straps, legs too. Now, in the unsympathetic fluorescent light of the hospital, Nate got a good look at Edgar's face. Ripped flesh, nodules of fat and dried skin, scraped bone and hunks of scabbed over gum line and jaw muscles. He eyes, though, were the worst. Wide globes, bloodshot and piercing, a thin, translucent eyelid occasionally swiping over them like a homeless man's rag on a luxury windshield. Teeth like a huge, horrific, unending grin, and the ragged edge behind the ear-line and up to the hairline, dried and shrivelling, and Edgar's black hair still slicked back from Brylcreem and dried blood.

"Edgar? I'm the guy you rescued a few nights ago. You know, from the rat things?"

Edgar's eyes darted over to him, panicking Nate for a second with the way they seemed to cut into his very soul. "Rat kids. I've been following them for a while now. Finally got one. Don't tell me, though. No body, right?"

Nate thought about it. He hadn't gone to the police with the attack. He barely believed it had happened himself, so explaining it to the police would've been futile. The hospital urged him to take his mugging claim to the authorities, but then there was the possibility of getting trapped in a lie. Nate decided that discretion was necessary and told no one, but Edgar was right. There was no body. Blood, yes, some of it his own, but certainly some of it was from the rat-like children that had attacked him, but the body was gone.

"Yeah, I can see it on your face. You don't know what the fuck you've gotten yourself into. Here. Undo my straps."

Nate initially moved towards the straps, then stopped. He looked at Edgar's mutilated face. Edgar looked at him. Then they both just stared at each other for a moment, each deciding what to do next.

"Fuck," Edgar said, breaking the silence, "you know I don't need to be strapped in. You owe me."

Nate ran a million scenarios through his head in a second and a half, many of which involved Edgar leaping out of bed, cutting Nate's face off and wearing it as his own, but against his better judgement, he quickly fumbled with the buckle until one arm was free.

"Thanks, brother," Edgar said, unbuckling the strap on his other arm before bending and working on the one on his legs. "I don't know if we got a proper introduction. Edgar Catafalque." Free from the restraints, Edgar uneasily stood up, wavered a bit from lightheadedness, and then stuck out his hand to shake Nate's.

"Nate Crossfield," Nate said, taking Edgar's hand in his own. The hand was surprisingly warm. Nate suspected it would be cold and corpse-like, but it wasn't. It was a firm, human handshake. "I'm a reporter." He'd said the words a hundred times before. A thousand. They always filled him with a sense of pride, and adventure. Now the very same words filled him with feelings of shame, of inauthenticity.

"Obscurologist," Edgar said. "I've seen things that'd straighten out your short and curlies. What rag do you work for?"

"The Real World Monitor."

"Ah," Edgar said, turning his attention back on Nate. He'd taken a moment to walk over to the small dresser in the corner of the room, and opened it up, revealing the bag containing his tan trench coat, the laundered white dress shirt and the rest of his clothes. "I suspected you were just a pawn, but the Real World Monitor, you're more enlightened than I thought you'd be. Interesting." Edgar pulled his black dress pants on under his hospital gown. "We Print News Other Papers Dare Not. Truer words were never written."

"I'm beginning to wonder if they understand what the word 'news' means."

"Bullshit. Big city newspapers are full of lies. Reporters are nothing but spin doctors for them, hiding the truth from the uneducated masses. The Real World Monitor. Now there's a paper that tells it like it is. You want to know what the newest mind control drug the military complex is feeding to the civilians to ensure their shadow dictatorship? You sure as shit ain't gonna find that in the Post! They censor anything that might jeopardize their hidden masters. No, the Real World Monitor has no agenda. Nothing to stop them from publishing the truth. You listen to me. It's the only paper you can trust."

Nate sat and ruminated on it for a moment. Edgar believed it. He and the other staff reporters, if you could even call them that, at the Real World Monitor made up a bunch of crap, took crackpot theories wholesale from the letter pile and published them as truths, and people like Edgar bought it. It changed the way Edgar viewed the world. Reinforced his own insane ideas instead of confronting the reality that no one is really in charge. That life is just a random bunch of meaningless events. Nate snapped out of it once he realized that Edgar was fully dressed and tying up his black dress shoes.

"Wait... what are you doing?"

"It's pretty self-evident. I can't stay here. I'm being hunted by groups more powerful and malevolent than your mind could possibly contain. They get to me... they learn the things that I know... and you can stick a fork in the ass of this planet. Doomsday. End of days."

"Where will you go?"

"I'm coming with you," Edgar said, standing up and brushing imaginary lint off of his pants. He reached into his pocket and pulled out his pack of cigarettes. Pulling one out and holding it in his bare teeth, he stood a moment and looked at Nate in the eye.

"Oh," was all Nate could muster.

17

The desert weasel is known for a few things. For instance, it survives in conditions that kill most everything else. Partially this is due to the massive amount it has to eat. Over the course of a couple days it has to eat its own body weight in food. While there are other desert rodents surviving off of insects, or even the sparse flora that exists in a desert, the weasel eats other rodents. Ground squirrels, mice, gophers, even the occasional rat. This survival instinct is so strong that it has evolved a kind of heartlessness towards its own kind, an inability to bond with other weasels that is unseen in many of the more evolved animals. It eats its siblings.

Another notable trait of the weasel is that they are vicious. They have been known not only to attack when cornered, but sometimes they attack for no apparent reason other than they just feel like attacking. They've attacked humans, been thrown off, and returned to leap at their throats.

The alien couldn't have known any of this as she walked through the desert. She saw the yellowish sun rise and set, rise and set, although the significance was lost on her. Her binary system, along with the off-kilter spin of her planet, allowed the habitable zones eternal daylight. Here, in the desert, she just knew the heat, and then the cold, the lightness, and then the darkness. For a woman as pale as she was, she should've been sunburnt bright red, unprotected as she was, but she wasn't. She was still pale, not pink nor red, not blistered nor peeling. She was just as pale as she was when she arrived in the desert days before. She was used to much more intense ultraviolet light.

If one had to guess, they'd probably peg her at about nineteen. They'd be wrong, of course, but that's the age she looked. Her long red hair reached all the way down her back, poker straight. She was skinny, so much so that at first glance you could see her ribs underneath her pale skin. It was hard not to notice many things her body as she walked, naked, through the desert.

That's when the small, furry weasel loped across the desert. The desert had surprised her with the variety of wonders previously unknown to her or anyone on her planet. Here there was rust coloured sand and dirt instead of the rich, fertile blue soil of her home, vegetation so varied in size and shape, unwilling to uproot and follow the rainclouds. Then the wildlife, each creature new and amazing. She'd seen desert birds, flapping so painstakingly to keep aloft in this heavy gravity, some following her in hopes that she may either have food with her, or drop dead from the heat, before they'd fly off disappointed. She stopped for a few hours to watch some desert beetles, spotted a few lizards, snakes, and in the evening, saw some bats flying overhead, the only creature that reminded her even slightly of home. The weasel came up close to her, sniffed at her foot.

Maybe her unfamiliarity, something odd about her physiology or residual orgone energy from the ship distracted the small creature, and she was able to reach down and pick it up. She looked at it, and it looked into her strange, aniridic eyes. For a brief moment, they connected. Two beings in a wasteland, both confused by the strangeness of the other.

Then she swiftly bit the head off the weasel.

"Hey!" a voice cried out from the distance. She looked across the open space to a man. He was running towards her, waving his arms. He was a small man, wearing a white lab coat with crusty red stains up the sleeves and across the chest. He was carrying a briefcase.

"Oh, thank God! Thank God!" Dr. Tarentola said, approaching her. She continued chewing the weasel head. It was much more difficult to eat than she had expected. He looked her up and down, confused by her lack of clothes, but desperation pushed him forward. "I've been stuck out here for a week! My car broke down! I was on the back roads… and no one came by… so I started walking…"

Munch munch munch. She understood some of what he was saying. She'd learned English, although they didn't speak it at home. Her mother made her learn. She'd wanted her daughter to understand her culture and heritage.

"There's nothing back there… I've been walking for days…" he said, gasping for breath. His lips, once thick and moist, were chapped and dry, his bald head red and burnt. "Um… where are your clothes? Are you okay?"

She didn't answer. She inferred what the words meant, but didn't understand why he would expect her to be wearing clothing when the temperatures didn't dictate a need for them. She'd seen hotter days, and colder nights without discomfort, and there was no protective need for them that she could ascertain. So, with this understanding in her head, she believed the polite response would be none. She spat out the skull of the weasel. Most of the meat was gone from it anyway. It hadn't tasted like she had assumed it would, so she dropped the headless weasel to the ground.

Dr. Tarentola looked at it. Bloodied stump of a neck, and then up at the blood, still on her mouth and hand. "Uh… I'm just going to leave," he said, before backing up, palms raised to show no aggression, then turning and running away through the desert.

18

Deep in Nestorian, the secret city buried beneath the Vatican, deeper than the secret archives and the seventeen oubliettes, Michael dodged and weaved his way through the growing number of monks and priests, bishops, and altar boys, all busily moving, working, maintaining the machine that was the church. Huge censers billowed incense of myrrh, cassia, spikanard, and saffron up into the marble walled chamber. The colossal expanse, larger than most townships, stretched out before Michael with huge statues, obelisks, and the largest structure, far off and hard to see through the highly smoky air, in the dead centre of Nestorian, the giant golden pyramid. Above, a dark, unseen ceiling held up by thousands upon thousands of pillars the size of ancient redwood trees. Each pillar was inscribed with scripture and gospels, like The Apostles' Creed or The Seven Sacraments. Dancing to the funk playing inside his head, Michael accented his manoeuvres with a circle slide around sacrificial lambs, a hip thrust into a spin behind the Tarasque shepherds, the huge lumbering Tarasque, six-legged ox-like creatures with thick turtle shells, extinct everywhere except the underground city, bleating and stomping in anger as they passed by the ornate buildings and golden statues. Despite his joyous moves, his life-affirming dancing, he had a sense of dread. He had bad news.

"You, check on Abbadon's Locusts," the Pope yelled, tension evident in his voice. His tall mitre pushed forward on his head, a bead of sweat soaking into the white fabric. "And don't comb the stingers from their tails!"

"Your Holiness," Michael said in his delicate voice, "your Papal tunic has been laundered and polished, restitched with consecrated thread. Winged cherubic virgins are manning the carriage in preparation, and three Agnus Dei will be accompanying you."

Michael paused. He was hoping the Pope would allow it to pass. Three Agnus Dei. Not four. The moment hung in the smoky air as the Pope looked up, pondering what he said next.

"Three?"

"Yes, your Holiness. I'm sorry. Three."

"Four!" the Pope suddenly raged at him. All activity halted immediately, all sound, even the shrieks of the tortured doves, silenced. The Pope leaned in close to Michael's highly sculpted face, his forehead nearly touching Michael's own cross-stamped forehead. "I demanded four! What is the problem!"

"I'm... I'm ready, as is Elvis and JFK, but it's the new one. Joey Ramone."

The Pope reared back, jaw set like steel, as he pulled his arms back, fists balled as if ready to hit whoever was closest to him. He restrained his urges and turned back to Michael. "What is the problem?"

"He just won't listen to anyone. Broke a bottle over St. Germaine's head. He... he called me a useless shitbag."

"Bastard! I knew these new performers were crap! Redeemers are picking any souls they want now. No sense of propriety. We used to have soldiers, warriors, goliaths. Now we get pop stars and punk rockers."

"Celebrities have huge egos. It gives them the ability, and often the motivation, to return. Normal people either are happy in death or are already haunting their houses. It's easiest to bring in the ones that crave the most attention."

"Yeah, and now we have fucking Andy Warhol walking around like he owns the place. Hey, is Oliver North dead yet?"

"I don't believe so, no."

"That's what we need. Not musicians. Soldiers!"

"I'm certain the three of us..."

"Silence! Fucking silence! I need four! Four Agnus Dei!"

"Your Celestial Purifier," Michael interjected, "we have the Antiquated Ones. They're resting in the necropolis. We could dig them up..."

"Fine!" the Pope hollered violently at Michael. "Do it. Get the Stigmatics to help you. They just sit on their asses moaning and bleeding all day anyway. And melt that Joey Ramone down to be reused, just like we did with Freddie Mercury. Fucking Redeemer idiots."

With a serious intention, the Pope strode through the sea of people, parting them like the Red Sea, as he headed for a baroque archway leading into the tunnels of the catacombs. Michael followed, rushing, flanked by two bishops entirely covered in heavy vestments. They were low-level bishops, not ready for battle, but more like a squire to a knight, following along behind the Pope readying him for the journey ahead. One held out a bladed crosier for the Pope to take, the long staff sitting delicately upon the bishop's outstretched hands. It was completely ignored by the Pope. The other, face fully covered by the black material of his hood except for thick leaded prescription glasses, attempted to wrap the spiritually armoured cloak over the Pope's shoulders like a cape. He, too was ignored by the Pope.

"I've still been unable to pinpoint the ecumenical cartogram. Have the virgins heard anything?"

"Not to my knowledge, your holiness."

"One touch... one touch and we'll know..."

They moved swiftly through the dark corridors, wax candles on the floors and the few sconces faintly lit, turning left and right, footfalls echoing off the marble floors and into the endless halls until the corridor opened into another chamber. Here, the air was free of smoke, and a sliver of natural light from a crack high above sliced down through the dusty air. In the middle sat the Pope's ceremonial chair, golden, encrusted with rubies and silver filigree, spiked along the outside of the enclosed chamber. Horizontal poles, polished mahogany outstretched from the front and back of the chamber, set for the four carriers to hold it aloft. At the end of each pole, a carrier stood. Young boys, all four of them, oiled and wearing only loincloths, but most impressively, a single large wing protruding from the shoulder blade of each, left wings for the boys on the left side, right for the right. The opposite shoulder blades, though, were scars, roughly stitched, where once another wing had extended majestically.

"At your word, your Holiness," Michael whispered.

Hours later, in the catacombs own burial grounds, the Stigmatics, blood dripping down their white robes, finished digging in the plots, surrounded by the towering wooden crosses with crucified immortal souls impaled at hand and foot upon their rough splintered wood. The Stigmatics, each one with tears of blood streaming down their stitched eyes, pulled the casket from the hole in the rocky earth. Wrenching at the lid, nailed shut decades earlier, some used their shovels, others yanked with bloody fingernails until the rusted nails finally gave.

The Agnus Dei, waxen, cross stamped deep into its forehead, lay motionless, military uniform covered in a layer of dust, dark hair and moustache shaved at the edges still perfectly preserved. Suddenly, abruptly, the Agnus Dei opened its eyes.

"Gott im Himmel!" it spoke.

19

"So, I don't know how to ask this, so I'll just ask it. What happened to your face?" Nate asked on the hour long drive back to Red Valley, landscape barren except the desert bushes, rocky ridges and red desert boulders.

"Plastic surgeon stole my face," Edgar grunted, then laughed his hoarse, throaty laugh, "how's that for a headline?"

"A plastic surgeon stole your face? I mean... why?"

"I could think up a hundred reasons. Maybe he was being paid by the Odd Fellows, Ordo Templi Orientis, Trilateral Commission, or a hundred others I could name. Maybe he's a collector, or maybe he's using the faces to put on robots. Hell, for all I know there could be a dozen clones walking around right now, claiming to be Obscurologists. Strong cells in the face. Good for DNA harvesting."

"What the hell? Why did you go to him in the first place?"

"Desperation, mostly."

It was well past dinnertime by the time the red Miata finally approached the small town. The car, once pristine, taken for a wash weekly in the city, was now caked in the dust of the desert with splatters of insects across the hood and windshield. The top was up, which was uncommon for Nate, as he loved the feeling of wind in his hair. With Edgar sitting beside him, faceless, exposed muscle and tendon, Nate decided the best plan was to keep the top latched tightly, even with Edgar smoking the entire way. Nate wanted to cover themselves as much as possible from onlooking eyes. Not that there was any other passable route than the desolate desert roads. Red Valley was remote, and on the trip to Pronghorn Mesa on the road that everyone called 'the main road' they still hadn't encountered a single other car. For all his childhood, he'd never been to the ones they called 'the back roads.'

After the conversation about Edgar's missing face dried up, Nate wondered what more to ask, half-worried that he'd say the wrong thing and half-knowing that there wasn't anything he could say that would fluster Edgar. Edgar lost his face, but after a few minutes of silence, Edgar puffing away on a cigarette, smoke escaping through his cheekless grin, Edgar turned and dug around in the back seat, found a copy of The Real World Monitor. He'd flipped to the back pages, past the articles claiming that Ronald Reagan was a "transvestite," Bigfoot migrations, and the baby born with a clock face instead of a normal face, to the advertisements at the back. He pulled a stubby pencil and dog eared notepad from his pocket and started scratching away.

"What on earth are you doing?" Nate said, trying to keep his eyes on the road. The featureless landscape dulled his senses, but luckily he still felt a stab of pain from the back of his leg to shock him into alertness.

"Resupplying."

Nate sat and stared at the road for a moment, the answer not clarifying the situation in any way. He hesitated a moment, wary that any explanation of Edgar's actions would result in the same lack of actual information. "Resupplying what?" he finally asked.

"I need tools. See here? Voodoo dolls, five for a dollar," he said, opening the paper for Nate to look at, which he didn't. "I haven't had voodoo dolls for years. Hard to get real ones. Most places sell them, and they don't do anything. Ones from the Real World Monitor, though, they're the real shit."

"Sure."

"Bless Me Jesus Spray," Edgar continued, "almost out of that. Blessing in an aerosol can. Necronomicon spell book, herbal erection pills… not that I need those… crystal balls, authentic Angel feathers. You can find everything here."

The trip continued in silence after that, Edgar making small grunting noises whenever he found something of interest and then scratching it down in his notebook. He only put the pencil and book away once they reached the twists and turns of the streets in the small town.

"Library's closed," Edgar said, noting it as they passed by.

"Yeah, it has been for a few days."

The car pulled up in front of the house Werner once owned. One thing was different, though. All the furniture that had been cluttering up the front of the yard was now gone. Nate knew that Brooke had been looking into finding people to drive it to the dump, but he'd thought she'd been unsuccessful. Apparently, she wasn't.

"Now, Edgar, maybe you should stay here for a moment. Let me clear it with Brooke. She doesn't really like surprise guests."

"Especially a guy with no face?"

"I think she's come to terms with that, after I got attacked."

"Come to terms with it, heh," he said, a smile would've graced his face, had he had one, "even I haven't done that. You go check with the missus. I'll be here."

Nate closed the Miata door behind him and started walking up to the front door of the house when Edgar's throaty, raspy voice called to him.

"Nate!"

"What?"

"I just wanted to…" Edgar said through the rolled down window of the Miata, "I wanted to say thanks. I know this is weird for you. I know you're not used to this sort of thing, but I just need a couple of days to get my head together. Get some clues as to where my face is."

"Your face? You mean you want to…"

"Well, yeah. What the fuck do you think I'm going to go. I have to get my face back."

"Uh…"

"So thanks. I'll only be a day or two. I'll find something."

"Okay… sure, man.

Nate turned and walked up to the front door, noticing the scrape marks on the hard ground where his father's furniture had been dragged away. A pang of guilt hit him. He should be visiting his father more. Maybe his father didn't deserve to be visited, and maybe he'd been a distant, unfeeling and often abusive prick throughout his childhood, but the memory of that old, frail man in the hospital still haunted him. He couldn't keep his anger, his bitterness. With the loss of the furniture came some relief that so much of his past was gone. He hoped it would never return.

"Brooke?" he said, opening the door. He walked in, and she wasn't in the kitchen. He'd half-hoped that she would have cooked dinner for him. After discovering the health food store in Pronghorn Mesa, her hatred for Red Valley had quelled slightly, and deep down he wanted a new start with her. She had her lunches of organic avocados sprinkled with chia seeds or kale and soya cheese on ancient grain bread. Nate hoped that finding her comfort foods would signal an acceptance of the small desert town.

Brooke often took naps throughout the day, sometimes just after lunch, sometimes later, so coming up the stairs and seeing the bedroom door closed wasn't out of the ordinary.

When he opened the door, though, it was out of the ordinary.

Moans and grunts, the bed squeaked and banged against the wall as Stan thrust himself deeper and deeper into Brooke, her fingernails dragging roughly across his back.

"What the fuck!" Nate yelled, loud enough to be heard over the gasps of passion. Stan rolled off of Brooke, pushed off.

"Nate!" Brooke screamed.

Nate grabbed Stan's overalls, crumpled on the floor, and threw them at him. "Get the fuck out of my house!"

"Well," Stan said, standing up. He was still erect, and easily twice the length of Nate. Not only was he muscular, toned, but also well endowed. Stan seemed calm, though. "I guess it's time to leave." He held the overalls in his hand as he walked, fully naked, from the room. "Neighbour," he said, nodding as he walked past.

"Nate! I'm sorry!" Brooke pleaded, holding the thin sheet up to cover herself. Nate wasn't seeing her though. He was seeing Stan's body thrusting on top of her. He was seeing his boss walking down the hallway doing up his pants. He was seeing smeared lipstick. "I never meant to…"

"You said you'd never do this again!" Nate yelled, voice wavering with fury. "You begged to come back to me! You begged for forgiveness, and I was the idiot that forgave you! And you fucked it up again!"

"It was just a moment of weakness! It was this stupid fucking town you dragged me to! I was lonely! I have nothing to do all day!"

"Get a fucking job! Help me out here for Christ's sake!"

"Get a fucking job?" Brooke yelled back, standing and wrapping the sheet around her, "what fucking jobs are there in this shit hole! Your job pays crap, and I'm supposed to wait tables or clean houses? You asshole! What kind of a man are you?"

"So it's my fucking fault you had to fuck the neighbour! You always fucking do this! You turn it on me! You make it my fault, even when there's no fucking way it's my fault!" His voice was cracking. He fought back with Brooke, sure, but not like this, not with the red hot rage behind his eyes, not with everything that she'd ever done to him, ways she'd made him feel inadequate and useless, all running through his head. The coldness, the distance, the complete lack of empathy and compassion. His voice rose. "You did this! You got us here! You!"

"You lied."

"Yeah, I lied. I lied before too, and I never got caught, because I'm smart, you fucking idiot! I'm smart, but I got caught because of you!"

"What the fuck are you talking about?"

"I implicated my boss. I wrote that he was being bribed by the mayor not to report on the conditions at the jail. I wanted to fuck that guy up so bad, and it's because you had to go and fuck him! You fucked everything up for both of us! You're to blame!"

"Oh, grab some fucking balls. Take some responsibility for your actions," she sneered.

Nate had his hand up to his mouth, fingers curving around the childhood scar on his face. He was breathing deeply, eyes staring deep in concentration. His next words would be key.

"Fine. Get out," he said, seriously, finality in his voice.

"What?"

"Get the fuck out of the house! Get the fuck out of Red Valley, and get the fuck out of my life!"

"Gladly!" Brooke yelled. Nate turned and stormed down the stairs, stopping to lean against a doorframe and catch his breath. He'd spent so long wanting her back, not the woman that Brooke had turned into, but the one in the apartment above the fish market. He'd wanted macaroni and cheese dinners by candlelight, late night walks through the park because they didn't have the money to go to a movie. He'd wanted the woman who made do with what he was able to provide. He looked out the front window and saw Edgar playing with the convertible roof of the Miata, but before he had a chance, Brooke came stomping down the stairs. She had pulled on a pair of designer jeans and a tan blouse, suitcase in one hand, dragging one of her many unpacked boxes of clothes with the other.

"And if you think I'm coming back to this pathetic town again you can get fucked!"

"I'm not asking you to!"

Brooke yanked open the front door, struggled with the box for a moment. Nate, for once, didn't try to help her. She dragged the box and suitcase out to the car, where Edgar looked up from playing with the buttons.

"Get the fuck out of the car!" Brooke yelled, throwing the suitcase in the back of the car, followed closely by the box. "Goddamn circus freak!"

Edgar and Nate stood at the front of the house, watching Brooke peel out, back tires spitting rocks and leaving parallel black streaks on the pavement.

"I judge by the naked man," Edgar said, hand on Nate's shoulder, "things didn't go well."

20

The pale woman walked silently through the darkness of the desert night until she came to the Impala. She had no frame of reference for such a thing, but she could ascertain its purpose. Four wheels, seats, it was obviously a land vehicle. Why it was half-straddling the obvious pathway was beyond her.

The desert heat wasn't the worst she'd experienced, but it was growing increasingly uncomfortable. For a few days, it was tolerable. Endearing, even. But lately, she felt it. She felt the sun's radiation beating down on her, the scalding earth beneath her bare feet. She would need nourishment soon, and moisture. Ending her visit early would be a failure, and it had taken so much to get her to the desert.

She studied the Impala. She ascertained that it had obvious corrosion on it, oxidization. In her mind she imagined that it had come from someplace where the atmosphere was more hydrated, like the eternally stormy moon around her own home planet. She squinted her eyes, fully encompassed in the darkness by her pupils. Black tires, yellow body, transparent windscreens.

Then, two lights appeared in the distance. They were approaching at great speed down the dirt road. She waited, watching them come closer, and when they came near, she stepped out to interact with them.

With a screeching of tires, followed by a crash that echoed through the empty desert landscape like thunder, the red Miata careened into the Impala, fibreglass exploding from the impact, followed by a rain of women's clothing from the back seat of the car. She stood, looking at them as they drifted to the ground, Versace blouses, Valentino gowns, Dior lingerie. Had she had a context for what she was seeing, she might have considered the experience surreal, but in a situation like hers, everything seemed surreal.

"Oh my god..." Brooke said, stumbling out of the wreckage, a gash on her forehead where she hit the windshield. The glass was shattered, marked with a star shape from the impact where her head hit. It happens only when a person isn't wearing a seatbelt, and Brooke had been so upset she'd forgotten all about putting it on. The wound itself was superficial but was bleeding terribly, blinding her in one eye as it flowed down the left side of her face and onto her blouse. "What... what happened?"

The pale girl studied Brooke. Her English was advanced enough to understand the question, but phrasing things appropriately was difficult. "My car broke down! I was on the back roads... and no one came by..." the alien said, repeating words, stolen from the man in the desert, complicated enough to sound authentic. The words felt strange in her mouth. She was trying to mimic the accent of the man, but the syllables came out difficult to understand, vowels sounding rehearsed, her throat clicks distinct through the English words.

Brooke looked at the girl, squinting through the darkness, her head still thick with pain and shock. "Why are you naked?" she asked, but it was too difficult to comprehend if she'd even asked the question appropriately, her head spinning and everything feeling foreign. She knew that she was only an hour or two out of Red Valley. She'd made a wrong turn leaving town, but the back roads all led to the same place eventually. For Brooke, that place was anywhere except Red Valley. She looked down at her clothes, spread out on the dirty road. "My clothes..." she said. She knew she'd have to get somewhere soon. The desert would kill her. She was already craving water, and it wasn't even daytime. "Cold... have to stay on the roads..." she mumbled through her haze, and then she left the pale, red-haired woman. She attempted to walk back on the road, but shock had set in, and she mistakenly made off into the wide expanse of the open desert.

The pale woman watched her leave. She hadn't quite understood what had occurred, but when in a strange land, confusion becomes commonplace, so she turned her attention to the road, picking up a purple dress that had landed at her feet.

21

It was midnight, and Nate sat on the ground beside his father's rusted brown pickup. He was there, but his mind wasn't. Not really. It was all too much for him, and he felt like a spirit floating above his body while Edgar rummaged around inside of the old truck.

Ten years had gone by. Ten years since he'd met that hippie girl. They'd been at a coffee shop. There had been a girl with an awkward haircut playing guitar on a small stage, Lorna, who, as it turned out, had been a good friend of Brooke's. There had been a bunch of people sitting around talking over top of Lorna's singing. But not Brooke. Nate had paid for his latte, in a bowl, and had scanned around for a table. He had taken with him a copy of London Labour and London Poor by Henry Meyhew, hoping it would inspire him to write more articles. He'd been doing a lot of piecework, beat reporting, a job here and a job there. It had never been the dream, for sure. He had wanted to be a columnist at the time, maybe reporting on the local scene, maybe opinion pieces. Crime. Crime would have been good, following a single murder to its conclusion, breaking details. More often than not, though, he had been sent out when some World War Two vets were having a picnic, or to report on the local parade. But then, there in the coffee shop, book under his arm, hot latte in his hand, and no free tables, he had seen Brooke and the empty chair across from her.

He had bumped and wriggled his way through the cluster of mismatched chairs to hers, and then had leaned over so that she could hear him over the guitar player. She had smelled of patchouli, had long hair and wore a patchwork shirt.

"Hey, there aren't any free seats. Mind if I join you?"

"Hey man, sure," she had said, still watching the girl performing. Lorna had been singing Suzanne by Leonard Cohen, her voice breathy and the chords simplified to give an honesty to the song, get to the heart of it.

Nate had sat down, pulled out his book, and pretended to read, but couldn't. Between the music and the allure of Brooke, his eyes just ran over the words with none of them entering his mind.

"Hey! Shine the light over here. I can't see anything with you moving that thing around," Edgar's rough voice broke in, dispelling his fugue of memory. Nate jerked forwards, quickly sucked in a deep breath.

"Yeah… yeah," he said, picking up the flashlight and shining it into the cab of the truck. Edgar had managed to yank out a bunch of the wires from beneath the steering column. "Why don't we just take your car?" he asked.

"With chupacabra? Truck makes a better battering ram than a car," Edgar responded, keeping his eyes on the exposed wires. "Plus, your rust bucket might make it there and back. My rust bucket might not make it to the end of the block. Dammit! For every time I've needed to do this, it never gets any easier." In reality, Edgar had hot-wired three vehicles, and this was the first time he was doing it legally.

"You mean… my father's truck is more reliable than your car?"

Edgar ignored him and continued fiddling with the wired, yanking them roughly and stripping the wires with his exposed teeth.

"How did you learn this?"

"You'd be surprised what you pick up in my line of work."

"Yeah, I can believe it," Nate said, exhaling deeply, "working for the Real World Monitor, I may need to add a few skills to my skill set."

All those years ago there had been a gazebo in the park across from the coffee shop. Nate and Brooke had walked out there after the coffee shop closed, and sat. They'd been talking for hours about their future plans, problems with the government, music, art, love. They had passed a joint back and forth, both secretly focusing on putting their lips on the soft paper, where the other's lips had been only moments before. Maybe they hadn't looked like a matching set, Nate with his cardigan and button up shirt, Brooke with a flowing dress and wild hair, but in that moment, that night, that place, they were perfect.

The sweat had cooled on their bodies that night in Nate's cramped bachelor suite, his twin mattress and box spring set on the floor, three bookshelves, and cushions instead of a couch. There hadn't been enough room for both of them to sleep comfortably, but it didn't matter. They had held each other close, limbs entwined, until both succumbed to sleep.

Boom!

The engine of the brown pickup sputtered and backfired to life for the first time in years. A cloud of black smoke blew out of the tailpipe into the darkness of the yard illuminated only by one measly flood lamp on the front of the house.

"Gotcha, bitch!" Edgar growled in celebration. "Okay, grab what you need. I have to keep the engine revved or it'll die."

"I don't need much," Nate called while running back into the house. He grabbed his pad and a couple of pens. He grabbed his phone too. While there'd be no coverage out at the old army base, he could at least try to get some photos. When he got back to the truck, Edgar was still in the driver's seat, so he got in the passenger side. It didn't matter to him. Even if Edgar crashed the thing, he'd at least get some insurance money out of it. The truck had three wheels in the grave by the sound of the engine.

"You got something to protect yourself with?" Edgar asked, pulling out onto the road, clutch kicking and bucking the whole time, stirring up the dust inside of the cab.

"What, like a gun? Yeah, I'm going to become a big time chupacabra hunter. Maybe catch ourselves a few snipes along the way."

Edgar turned his bug-eyed gaze over to Nate. Nate looked back, remembering that he'd been attacked by rat kids, and was sitting in a truck with a man with no face.

"I should get a gun."

Years had passed. Brooke had changed after Lorna died. Lorna had liver cancer. It had been quick, but painful, and Brooke had held her hand day after day, watching her grow thinner and thinner until there was nothing left of her. Brooke then stopped burning incense, stopped smoking pot and had traded her sandals in for a pair of patent leather pumps. She had gotten a job as a temp, and then hired by the temp company to hand out jobs to other career seekers. After that, she had been headhunted by a gas company, life changing once again. Conservative haircut, lots of money, followed by a high-pressure supervisor, self-doubt, anxiety. Then, that was it. Career over as abruptly as it started.

Of course, Nate had gotten a few really hot leads, broke a few corrupt businesses, took down a local Alderman, and had gotten promoted further up, higher and higher. His name had become commonplace in the associated press, money had been rolling in, and people in high places were noticing.

What they had noticed was fearlessness. On paper, Nate had felt invincible. He could write anything, and people had listened. Some had attempted lawsuits, some threats, nothing had phased him. When the television news had called, he had accepted quickly, and when the news magazine programs called, he had stepped up the career ladder once again. Each opportunity that had popped up for him was just another line on his resume so soon he'd be behind the desk, anchoring the show. That had been the plan.

"Chupacabra sightings have been coming in since 1995, although I've heard of them coming through the occult underground since the fifties," Edgar grumbled. The drive out in the darkness wasn't long. Nate's father drove out to the base all the time, as did a hundred or so other military personnel. That had been years ago, though, before they pulled out, abandoned the base to the desert. "Nasty creatures. Vicious. I'm glad the Real World Monitor is finally looking into it. Public hazard." Edgar pulled through the abandoned gates onto the paved roads, covered in dust and earth from the years of neglect. Tire tracks, undoubtedly from teens racing their cars or finding it a convenient place to drink undisturbed, ran in ruts through the dirt.

"Don't be too glad. It's the Real World Monitor. No one believes this crap."

"You'd be surprised."

The base was like a small town of streets and avenues, one large building, three stories, brick, sitting right in the middle. Doors locked tight, but most of the windows were broken out. There were a couple dozen smaller buildings lining the streets, garages to repair the desert Jeeps, storage, barracks and canteens. There was even an old decrepit obstacle course with frayed ropes hanging from wooden structures, logs to run on, dirt pile taller than the building. Nate looked at the course, imagining his father as a young man, out there swinging and jumping and climbing. Nate could never have done it, and both Nate and his father had known it. Edgar pulled the truck up to the front doors of the building before the truck sputtered into silence. Nate looked at Edgar. They both knew how long it took to get it hot-wired to begin with, and they both worried that it'd take that long to restart it. If it restarted at all.

"Chupacabra," Nate said, "they're like, desert dogs with mange or something, right?"

"Oh yeah, just dogs. Puppies, really, if you want to believe that the mainstream mind washers want you to believe. You want to live your life thinking there's not much going on beyond the end of your nose. Sure, go back to watching reality television and eating sensory dulling fast foods."

"Edgar. That's just what I heard, man."

"Yeah. Okay, they're maybe related to canids, but I've never seen a dog the size of a bear. Never seen a dog with a row of spikes down its spine. You come face to face with one of these things, see their huge teeth bared, sharklike eyes staring at your neck, you'll wonder if they're canids. More likely descendants of Andrewsarchus or Borophagus mixed in with demonic influences. Probably."

"You know, my Dad worked in this building," Nate said as they rounded the corner of the building, checking doors and windows for entry, "but I never went inside. All hush hush. You know how the military always makes it out like they know all these things, but really, it was probably just organizing food shipments or ordering some helicopter part for the coast."

"No, that's what they want you to think," Edgar said, scanning out through the night, looking for any trace of movement. "They set up Area 51 as an alien research base. They'd contact aliens and then send a bunch of actors to look like kooks who make ridiculous contradictory claims. They get knocked down as crazies and meanwhile, the military maintains hidden in plain sight. Seriously fucked up, but it works. How many times have you seen someone claim to have seen aliens that doesn't look completely insane? I mean, I've seen aliens, so I know."

Rather than respond, Nate just kept looking around at the landscape. He shone his flashlight around at the big hill, in the windows of the small surrounding buildings, but he saw nothing.

Finally, certain that the evening was a total bust, he couldn't resist but yelling out into the desert, out of frustration, "Here Chupacabra! C'mon chupie chupi chupi!"

"Shut up!" Edgar yelled, but then a growl... an unearthly low pitched growl, distant but still fully audible, made its way across the open desert.

"Fuck was that?" Nate yelled. Then the stench hit them. It was unbearable, like wet fur and shit, like a skunk that fell into an outhouse hole, but a hundred times worse.

"Fuck you think?" They backed up against the building, Nate jerking his flashlight back and forth across the land, Edgar pulling a small Beretta subcompact pistol from his trench coat pocket. "We're too exposed out here, Nate. Get that door open."

Nate handed off the small flashlight, which Edgar held on top of his gun so he could see what he was shooting at, while Nate slammed his shoulder into the wooden back door of the building. He gasped for breath in the putrid air.

"Jesus, Nate! Kick, not shoulder, near the lock but not on it. You never kick a door in before?"

"Of course not!" Nate yelled back, looking over at Edgar, but instead, seeing a silhouette against the night sky. It was huge, eight feet tall, long wisps of hair dangling off of its raised arms.

"Guraaaaahhhhhhh!" the beast roared, guttural and deafening. Nate felt the roar in his bones, in his back teeth and his intestines. Edgar let off two shots into the darkness, cracking across the open desert, hitting nothing.

Nate kicked the door again, at the lock, back foot planted firmly and the weather exposed wood splintered and cracked. Nate yanked open the remains of the door and slipped through the opening, Edgar backing in as well, flashlight lurching across the land, finding nothing.

Then, the silhouette in the doorway, dwarfing it with its immense size.

"Raaahhhhhrrr!" the beast bellowed, and the flashlight caught a glimpse of brownish fur, ape-like fingers.

Crack! Edgar shot again, and the beast disappeared from the doorway.

In the darkness of the building, Nate huddled in a corner, pen held defensively. Upon reflection, Nate decided Edgar had been right about bringing something to protect himself with. The door had been a fire exit, and he was backed up against a row of lockers.

"Is it gone?" Nate asked, his voice wavering in fear.

"You feel like sticking your head out there to see?" Edgar asked, then grunted out a laugh.

"Holy shit, Edgar. What the fuck was that? Was that a chupacabra?"

"Nate, don't be ridiculous. Skunk ape, probably." Edgar handed back the flashlight to Nate, and as it jerked around in the darkness, Nate caught a strange, familiar sight. He shone the flashlight at the locker. Specifically, the name on the locker. W. Crossfield.

"Edgar... this is my father's locker," he said, dumbfounded. He'd known that his father worked in the building, but as he'd never been inside of it, there was still a part of him that didn't believe it. Now, confronted with the tangibility of a locker in front of him, reality set in.

"That's good. Now if we only had a crowbar we could look at his old undies."

"No... crap," Nate fumbled with the flashlight and pulling down the collar of his shirt to the key, still on the dirty string around his neck. It was the key that his father had given him, far too small to be the key to the pickup truck. He pulled it out, but not off from around his neck, and leaned in to slip the key neatly into the lock. It turned, hesitantly, rusted metal grinding on rusted metal, and clicked open. Nate pulled out the key and shone his flashlight into the nearly empty locker. At the bottom, a folded piece of old linen, yellowed and frayed at the edges.

"Anything interesting?" Edgar said, leaning in, wide eyes, skeletal grin.

"I don't know," Nate whispered, pulling out a decrepit piece of fabric. He unfolded it delicately, dust falling out in small puffs. On the other side, scribbles, black patches, some yellows.

"Looks like a map," Edgar said, peering at it over Nate's shoulder. He reached out a finger to point at a small glowing dot on the page. It seemed as though it was moving. "What's that?"

"It's moving..." Nate said, "it's in the fabric... but it's moving..."

And beyond the doorway, beyond the obstacle course and the big hill of dirt, the old grey-bearded man known as Umba hunched, talking to the large hairy creatures around him.

"We can't engage anyone," Umba said, his voice dry and parched from the laborious journey from the mountains into the desert.

"Uh uh... guh.." Cinnamon responded, her huge body and long limbs untouched by Edgar's bullets. Six other Bigfoot, the strongest warriors of the clan who'd been chosen to accompany Umba and Cinnamon, gathered around her, forming a protective circle in case they were attacked by the man with the gun.

"We're just here to watch. I'm sorry. I know it doesn't make sense, I feel something, but this isn't it. This isn't who I'm looking for," Umba said, sadness in his voice. "You can't risk yourself, Cinnamon. I don't want you to get hurt. These men, they have guns. They're dangerous."

"Gaaw," Cinnamon vocalized, putting her massive black hand on Umba's shoulder and pulling him close to her in a loving embrace.

22

It took Nate and Edgar three hours to get back on the road. Two of those hours were spent cowering in the abandoned military building, in the darkness, hoping that whatever it was, possibly a Skunk Ape according to Edgar, had left. The they spent another hour fiddling with the pickup truck, while Nate, Edgar's Berretta in one hand and the flashlight in the other, stood guard as Edgar coaxed the old truck to life. By the time they actually left the base, the sky was growing increasingly light with the approaching sunrise.

"...and then I was cornered. I knew too much about Mrs. Bush and her predilection for writing from the perspective of her dog. Either way, I barely got out of there with my life," Edgar said. He'd started talking about the links between Chupacabra and global warming, but the conversation veered around worse than his steering. Nate still wasn't feeling clear-headed enough to keep a vehicle on the road. The headlights illuminated the dusty roads through the waning darkness of the desert dawn. The back roads were empty. Not simply because of the time, but because most of them didn't lead to anywhere important. There were intersections between the meandering dirt roads, but they were few and far between, and the barren, rocky terrain made for few landmarks to navigate by.

Nate sat still for most of the conversation, still shell shocked by the events of the night, but at least listening to the strange rationality and bizarre tales helped to pass the time. "Early on in my reporting career," Nate said during the first sign of silence, "I was threatened. Almost got my ass kicked. I'd been investigating this local non-profit organization meant to help women in abusive relationships get to a shelter safely. You know, they have donations around the city, people throw their change in to help the women, that kind of thing." Nate paused for a moment, lost in the memory. It was a nice relief from the pressure of the day, the loss of Brooke. "I found out that over ninety percent of the profits went into the founder's accounts. She used it to build decks on her summer house, send herself and her two sons on retreats to Las Vegas, that sort of bullshit. I don't know. It seems like every non-profit has someone embezzling from it, but this one kind of hit home, you know?

"Well, before publishing the story, I go to their office to get her side of things. She's got these two sons, like, fucking white sumo wrestlers or something, and once I got in there they stood at the door, blocking me in, while the woman explained how it would be in my best interest not to publish the article. Now, this was still pretty early on in my career, and I'd been doing a lot of light hearted feel-good reports up to that point. Kite festival in the park kind of crap, so I'm totally unprepared for this. Then these two behemoths drag me out into the alley, and I'm shitting my pants at the point, but even they understood the power of the press, and let me go with just the threat that there would be more to come if I published the article. I did, of course, and never even saw those boys again, nor their mother. There were police investigations after that, and she was fined, but never saw jail time. I just wished that the fine went to a women's shelter instead of just the city's accounts, but the city wasn't any more interested in doing the right thing than she was. The money probably just built a deck for the chief of police instead."

"No skunk apes, though, eh?" Edgar laughed his throaty laugh.

"You got me there. No skunk apes, no goblins or little green men…"

"Grey."

"Yeah, no little grey men. Just thugs. Stupid humans."

"So, you all right? Edgar asked.

"Yeah, that thing out there just scared me. Everything is so weird, and then there's a hairy animal in the desert. It's all so unnerving."

"That's not what I'm talking about."

"Huh?" Nate asked, looking over.

"Your wife left you," Edgar said, his voice rough and gurgling, but still soft and sympathetic, "that's got to be hitting you. You looked like you were in a coma back at the house."

"I don't know, it's like… she's hated me for so long," Nate said, looking out of the windshield with glassy eyes, "it's awful to be with someone who hates you so much. Walking on eggshells all the time. She used to look at me with such confidence, like I could solve all her problems. Back when we first met I guess she just thought I was so much more impressive, you know? As the years went by, I just became normal. Just her plain old husband. She started solving her own problems, got a job that paid well, and I became… I don't know… just some idiot who didn't put his dishes away, or didn't fold the towels properly. Have you ever been married?"

Edgar chuckled to himself, not answering the question.

"Maybe it's just how things go in a marriage. It's like, I was the centre of her world, and then she changed, and I didn't belong in it at all. I was a relic of her previous life, an old car, and she wanted the newer model. And she cheated on me. Twice."

"That's harsh," Edgar said, keeping his bulbous eyes on the road ahead.

"Maybe if I'd only been a better damn husband, you know? Maybe it is my fault. If I'd been around more, did all those stupid things that they show on commercials at Valentine's Day. But I had to pay the bills, right? I had to..."

Screeech!

Nate's sentence was cut short as suddenly a woman appeared standing in the middle of an intersection. She was more of a blur as Edgar wrenched on the steering wheel, careening off of the road and into the creosote bushes lining the road. The creaky pickup truck came to a halt in a cloud of dust.

A moment passed while Edgar and Nate took in the situation in silence. Then Nate unhooked his seatbelt and jumped out of the truck. Edgar followed closely behind. They raced over to the woman, who was still standing directly in the centre of the two dirt roads. It was a pale woman, in a bright purple dress and bare feet.

"Are you all right?" Nate asked, running up to the road. Judging from the ruts dug up in the dirt, they very nearly hit the girl.

"There's nothing back there for miles..." the pale woman said, again reiterating phrases she had heard, although her mispronunciation of the vowels, deepening the 'a' into an 'o' sound as in the word 'walk,' and pronouncing every 'e' as a long vowel, sounding more like "bock theer for mils." There were also clicks in her throat, remnants of her native tongue.

"Listen to her voice, Nate," Edgar said, "look how pale she is. She's probably been stuck out here for days. She's not going to last another hour out here."

"Jesus, what happened to her?" Nate said, taking the girl's hand in his own. It was cold to the touch, but the desert gets cold at night. "Look, we're going to take you to town, get you some water, all right? Is that okay?"

"Yes," the girl said. She was a little proud of herself, and a smile emerged from the pallid corners of her mouth. She understood what he had said, and answered accurately. She looked at Edgar, his horrible visage, the red, pulpy muscles, the discoloured flesh and patches of fat and bone and cartilage. He was different than the other people she'd encountered.

"Thank you," she said in her odd accent. Edgar would've squinted, if he didn't have only a thin ribbon of ragged flesh for an eyelid over his bulging eyes, and instead just grunted.

"Which direction did you come from?" Nate asked, "Where is your car?

"My car broke down..." she continued, "and no one was coming..."

"You know what? Don't worry about your car," Nate said, guiding her to the truck. She moved well through the deserts shrubs, "we'll take care of that, or insurance will, or whatever. I know it's probably hard to think, but you need to get to town."

Edgar got into the driver's seat, and Nate helped the woman into the middle of the truck bench. It was only luck that the truck didn't flip in that wild lurching exit from the road, and even greater luck that the engine kept running. As Nate pulled himself up into the window seat of the truck, he got a better look at the woman under the interior lights of the truck. She had perfect porcelain skin and beautiful red hair, no makeup whatsoever, and there was something about her, maybe the way she held herself, maybe her confidence or her vulnerability that made her seem special, unique.

"Hey," Nate said, a realization hitting him, "my wife has a dress like that."

23

The following morning, Nate sat at his desk at the Real World Monitor, yawning. He'd gotten no sleep the night before, and not just because of his assignment at the old military base. After getting back to Red Valley and knowing that Dr. Bhijani was on vacation, they were concerned for the woman's safety, so they brought her to Nate's house. She drank water by the litre, and while Nate had prepared a broth for her, as he'd heard that people who were lost in the desert would throw up regular food until their stomachs became accustomed to it again, she ate ancient grain bread and soya cheese with no problems. Smiling even.

They'd put her up in Nate's old bedroom. Nate had gathered together all the blankets in the house and made a ramshackle mattress on the floor. He'd wished that Brooke hadn't thrown away all the furniture. A bed, even his kid's sized bed, would've been better than the pile of blankets, although the woman laid down on it, without taking off her dress, and fell fast asleep before Nate had left the room. He turned off the light but looked at her for a moment before shutting the door. He'd expected to be so alone tonight, so lost in his grief at Brooke's departure, but here he was, with two houseguests.

Edgar got stuck sleeping in the living room on the white B&B Italia sofa. He'd put a green garbage bag over the cushion in case his horrific wounds opened during the night and he'd bled all over it, and put a damp tea towel over his face. He was a bit too tall for the sofa, but it was probably nicer than the back seat of his Buick Wildcat.

"Late night, eh Scarface?" Mr. Leone said, his voice far too loud and jarring for so little sleep. Nate immediately put his hand up to the scar on his face, almost subconsciously. Every time Mr. Leone called him that, it irritated him just that much more.

"You could say that, Mr. Leone," Nate said, "went out to the army base last night. Chupacabra hunting."

"You went at night!?!" Mr. Leone said, a guffaw escaping his large mouth, "are you crazy! You should've gone in the morning! You could've taken the day!"

"My life has been difficult lately. My wife left me."

"Oh. Nate," he said, his voice soft as he used Nate's actual name for the first time since they met, "I'm really sorry, buddy. You need a few days for yourself? We got your covered here at the paper." Dasha walked over to Nate and put her hand on his shoulder. She was wearing a dark blue dress and matching headwrap, rhinestones across the fabric like constellations in the night sky.

"Nate," Dasha said, her voice sorrowful," I'm so sorry for you."

"Thanks, Dasha, Mr. Leone. I appreciate it. I think I'll just keep working. That's kind of why I went out last night. I don't want to sit around the house moping and crying all day. I'll deal with it, but working just gets my mind off of things."

"Lordy, I hear you. I'm divorced. Three times. None of them stayed. No, it's not easy to be the wife of a newspaperman."

"I guess, to be honest, I kicked her out."

"No," Mr. Leone continued, leaning his ample mass against a filing cabinet, his white dress shirt pulling up to expose the bottom of his belly, "can't blame them for leaving. Always on a new article, always off on a new adventure, and they're left at home. I couldn't imagine the boredom they must face waiting for us."

"That really wasn't the case for me."

"Flights off to Alaska, or the Congo, late night stakeouts finding the perfect source, tracking down leads for days on end. It's tough on a marriage. All my wives misunderstood it. They just thought I was being... what was the term they all used... emotionally unavailable... a bad listener... stuff like that, but no, it was the job. I feel for you, my boy. It ain't easy."

"She slept with the neighbour."

Dasha gasped and looked over at Mr. Leone, who was already looking out the window at someone passing by.

"Oh, hey... how did that chupacabra lead work out anyway? Anything come of it?"

Nate sighed. "No, not unless they're eight feet tall, hairy, and smell like a skunk."

"Maybe reared up a big one could be that tall, but hairy? Smelly? No, you're dealing with some kinda big hominid. Maybe a Mapinguari. Had a sighting of a Mapinguari a few years back. Turned out someone was driving through town with one of those Newfoundland dogs. Poor thing. Who brings a dog like that to visit the desert. Either way, doesn't sound like Chupacabra to me, but we need something for the article. Write down what might have happened had there been a Chupacabra there, and we'll figure out the logistics later. Mapinguari-Chupacabra war! Yeah, that's gold!"

"I'll report what people report to us, even if I don't believe it, but I'm not just going to make up facts. I told you that."

"Yeah, you said that," Mr. Leone said, laughing so loud that even the writers on the other side of the room looked up.

"Har har har!" Hardy chimed in, although he didn't even actually hear what Nate had said. It was just a knee jerk reaction. After twenty years at the Real World Monitor, Hardy knew the path of least resistance.

"I'll expect it on my desk by the end of the day! Ha ha ha!" Mr. Leone said, laughing as he lumbered back to his office.

"You do it," Dasha advised him, "you do it, don't think about it. Just do it and keep going. It's going to be all right."

Nate sat at the keyboard to his antiquated Macintosh computer. His arms felt heavy as his mind raced. This was his life now. Lies. His career had started so authentically, so ready to expose truths, but getting there something happened somewhere, some change, likely something small to start it rolling, maybe a quote that a person said changed slightly for dramatic effect, maybe a detail he'd invented to evoke some response from the reader. Then whole quotes, changes in the facts of the story, and then implicating his employer in a poorly thought out revenge scheme. Lies. All of them lies, including the biggest one, himself. He lied to himself about who he was, about the kind of person he was. He always thought of himself as the hero of his own story, but he was sneaky, cowardly, willing to live in a loveless marriage instead of finding true love. Now it was all unravelling, and he was seeing who he really was. The kind of guy who works at the Real World Monitor, getting paid crap wages to make up bullshit stories for bored losers and conspiracy nuts.

He slammed his fist down on the keyboard, resolute that this was going to change. He wasn't going to be this person. He was going to change his life.

Then he remembered what he had to do, like getting a car. Brooke had taken the Miata and left, not looking back. He needed to fix up the house before selling it, as if anyone would even want a collapsing house in a dying desert town. He'd already lost everything. It was over.

'Chupacabra Fight' he typed on the computer, silently protesting every keystroke. Thankfully, a scream outside the office building stopped everyone typing. The door to the office opened, and Edgar, facial bones and musculature open for all to see, bloody stain on the collar of his freshly laundered dress shirt, came in. The office halted completely. Reporters stood up at their desks to watch the pulp-faced man at the door. One woman in the office, who Nate was introduced to on his first day and promptly forgot her name, was, unluckily enough, standing directly in his path and immediately fainted, straight to the floor. Edgar deftly stepped over her, still scanning the room for his friend.

"Nate!" Edgar said, spotting him at his keyboard, "I got something!" Edgar manoeuvred through the file cabinets and desks, apologizing to the writers as he bumped into their desks, spilling piles of papers off the cabinets as he made it to Nate. He slammed the map down in front of him. "Look at this!"

The map looked different. Last night at the military base, it looked like it was printed on dark cloth, almost black, but now it looked bright, the linen fabric a light tan colour.

"Aren't you supposed to be at my house with that woman? Is she all right?"

"Oh, she's fine. Still sleeping last I looked," Edgar said dismissively. "We got hoodoos here, dried out river down here," he said, darting his finger over the map faster than Nate could see what he was pointing at, "and here, look at this symbol. Only one on the map."

"Nate!" Mike Rant yelled from his desk. He was the only one who hadn't stood up, the only one who kept working while everyone else was losing their minds over the faceless man. "Keep it down, for Christ's sake! This piece on drug using communist welfare dregs isn't going to write itself!"

Nate looked at the map closely, ignoring Mike Rant completely. The images were strange, almost luminescent, dark patches looking like cloud cover, but that didn't make sense to him, as who would put cloud cover on a map? But there was definitely a symbol in the desert. It looked like a letter 'P' with a longer stem, with a letter 'X' intersecting the bottom half. Then, in the spaces on the sides of the 'X' were an Alpha symbol on the left, and Omega symbol on the right.

"That's the Chi Ro symbol. It's religious."

"Aren't you trying to track down the surgeon who stole your face?"

"Move over," Edgar said, hustling Nate off of his seat and pulling the map off of the keyboard where he had placed it. "Holy shit, Nate, what the fuck is up with this computer? Does it even get internet?"

"Barely."

"I think we might have better luck hooking this keyboard up to a rock," he said, tapping away at the keys rapidly, using only two fingers on each hand yet still maintaining a quick pace. "Look here, East of town a few hours. Hoodoos, river here, probably dried out at this time of year. This is the place!"

"So?"

"So! This map... haven't you noticed that it changes! Haven't you seen that the clouds are moving across the land!" Edgar yelled, and then looked around at the other reporters all still watching the unbelievable scene before them. "Go back to work, people! What, are they paying you to gawk at me?"

Nate took a close look. The fibres of the map did appear to be changing colour, if only slightly, giving it the appearance that the clouds were moving. And he had to admit that it did appear darker the night before when the land itself was dark.

"The little light we saw on the map last night, you remember? The glowing dot? That was a car on the highway. It was visible on this map. This map is changing in real time. Now there's a symbol on the map with religious significance, and you're just sitting there saying 'so?' We have to check this out!

"Yeah," Nate said, exhaling deeply and looking at the two words he'd typed on his computer screen. Chupacabra Fight. "Not like I have anything better to do."

24

"For the love of God, please…" the disembodied voice called out. It had been getting worse and worse, louder over time, Phaedra thought. Perimeter checks around the crumbling shack had stopped entirely now, and Phaedra spent most of her days doing anything she could to keep the voices out of her head. She'd read her books, twice each, although it was more like looking at words, as the voices caused so much of a distraction that whenever she started getting into the plot, she was immediately withdrawn from it by cries of torment or fury. She scoured every word and image in her vintage wrestling magazines, anything to try to distract herself.

"Hate you! Hate you all!" another voice cried. Phaedra cleaned her boots with intensity, hoping that her concentration would block out the voices. It didn't.

Rations were holding out well, although Phaedra was barely eating. If there's something to be said for the military, they don't want you starving to death. They went above and beyond in stocking the fridge, although maybe they realized that finding someone else willing to guard a shack in the middle of the desert was unlikely, and they'd already resigned themselves to stranding Phaedra out there. Phaedra had started thinking that Colonel Nine would never actually return and that her food and water would run out, or her sanity.

Time was getting more and more difficult for her to discern. She'd been waking in the night, disoriented, getting dressed like it was morning when the sun hadn't even tinted the horizon. She'd been forgetting to eat, to drink. She'd once attempted to walk to the shack and found herself hiking through desert brush, the shack ten minutes behind her. Even sitting in the tent, stars circled the edges of her vision.

She stood up, blackness clouding her peripheral vision. She reached for the satellite phone. Nine would have to get her. She succumbed. She gave up. For a moment Phaedra wondered if that's what Nine wanted all along. She put the phone to her ear and prepared to dial, but someone was already on the line.

"Corporal Phaedra Wilson," the monotone voice said. "You were told not to use this phone."

"I need help," Phaedra pleaded, "the desert… there's voices…" Her voice cracked from the dry desert air.

"Corporal Wilson. Your distress has been noted. Please state the nature of your emergency."

"I can't take it anymore... I'm hearing voices... seeing things... I'm losing my mind out here."

"Unless there is a physical and immediate threat, I cannot approve any action. Please return to your post. When there is available and appropriate support for the site, you will be informed. Do not use this phone again. The airwaves are monitored by our enemies."

"Wait a second," Phaedra said, suddenly recognizing the voice at the other end of the phone, "Colonel Nine?"

The phone went dead. Phaedra turned it off and on again, but no dial tone came from the receiver, no amount of button pressing or shaking would place any further call. She lay down on the cot again, her hand grasping the rail as the world suddenly became dizzy again.

Her mind wandered back to that small diner in that crappy little town. Greasy eggs over easy with hash browns. Real hash browns. Potatoes, diced and fried in the kitchen, not taken from some freezer and thrown on a grill or deep fried. The rations were adequate, thanks to the refrigerator hooked up to the solar panels. She'd lived off of C rations before, but after a few weeks of it, it was nearly intolerable. It was nothing like fresh cooked food, even from a greasy spoon like the Lucky.

"Sinners and Saints alike..." a voice called out.

"I just want to know if she's all right," another voice cried into the empty desert.

The afternoon was hot, like every afternoon. Phaedra spent the afternoons in the shade of the tent. There were ice packs in the freezer which she saved for late afternoon when the heat was at its most sweltering. She'd been posted in the swamps of Florida, but it never felt as hot, even though the humidity was insufferable. But here, the spikes of heat contrasted by the frigid nights, was the worst she'd ever had it.

"Never told us..."

"Son... are you there... is that you..."

Phaedra was an excellent soldier. She followed orders when others went running for cover. She took on jobs, like the one cleaning radioactive waste that irradiated her own skeleton, that others would rather go to the brig over than expose themselves to. Not Phaedra. Maybe it was her upbringing, her family's military history, or maybe it was her own stubbornness that there was nothing she couldn't do, but she never turned down an assignment.

She didn't have to be there. She didn't have to follow the family tradition of joining the military. Her three brothers had already kept the tradition alive, so no one would have faulted her for following a different path. She could've gotten a job anywhere and been treated better. She could have worked at the hardware store. It was just down the block from her parents' house, and she knew the owner. She could've gotten a job in an office, or flipped burgers, or washed cars. Anything. Or, and the thought surreptitiously entered her mind like it usually did, followed her passion for professional wrestling. She could've put on the colourful spandex tights, lightning bolts or fireballs down the legs, maybe pulled a mask on her face like the Lucha Libre do. She could've strutted around the ring, chest out, slamming her opponent's head into the turnbuckle. At the end, they could've interviewed her as she held the oversized leather and metal belt over her head and challenged all her competitors to take it from her. End of the day, she;d buy a round of beer for them all, "allies" and "enemies" alike, and join the camaraderie of the group.

No, Phaedra was a soldier. A faithful and obedient soldier. But something snapped.

Maybe it was the heat. Maybe it was the constant voices in the desert, calling her and berating her, waking her in the mornings and calling to her late into the night. Or maybe she'd just endured enough abuse from the military, her eagerness to please the higher ranks taken advantage of for the last time.

"Fuck it."

She got up from her tent and, once again feeling light-headed at first and a moment of tunnel vision as the stars shooting across her vision, left the shade and walked to the shack. Options were scarce. She could've just started walking out into the desert, looking for signs of life, of civilization, but Phaedra knew that wasn't going to happen. She'd die well before then. The trip out to the base had been long and desolate, and going back on foot was not at all possible. Another phone call would be equally as useless. The only other possibility that came to Phaedra's mind was to break into the shack, see if there was anything in there that could help her. Hell, even if she just figured out the significance of what she was guarding maybe it would ease her mind from the auditory hallucinations she'd endured nonstop for days.

The shack really was nothing to look at. Dried boards, greyed with age, nailed haphazardly together, door chained with a rusty lock. Phaedra hesitated, looking at the grey planks of the door, the loose screws in the hinges. A memory spoke in her head, a familiar voice. Someone tries, someone dies. Phaedra mustered her remaining strength and gave it one swift kick with her tan army combat boot. The hinges gave way to cracking wood, and a cloud of dust billowed out as the door fell inward. She bent over and pulled the busted door from the shack and threw it behind her. Her hands shook, as did her knees. She hadn't anticipated how much strength she'd lost due to exposure. She wasn't even sure how long she'd been out in the desert any longer.

The interior of the shack mirrored the exterior in its rough appearance. The rugged, untreated grey wood held nothing. Nothing was hung on the walls, and for some reason, Phaedra expected to see something like rakes or other gardening tools, but suddenly realized how ridiculous that would have been.

Instead, there was only one thing inside of the shack other than the bare bulb hanging from a cord overhead. A barrel. Blue paint was peeling off of the rusty metal, and the words '55 US Gal' was stamped into it on one side, Product of Jordan stamped on the other.

Phaedra stood there in amazement. She'd spent countless days looking at a shack, endured both visual and auditory hallucinations. After a dumbfounded moment, Phaedra yanked on the lid, pulling it off and dropping it with a clang to the floor.

She dipped her finger in the black liquid inside the barrel. Oil.

"All this effort... all of this torment and heat and solitude," she said aloud, rubbing her fingers together, the slickness of the black liquid slippery between them, "for a fucking barrel of oil."

25

The old brown pickup truck lurched to a halt, sputtering and coughing before the engine finally stopped spitting out black smoke. Nate pushed open the creaking door, stepping down onto the hard packed earth that was his front yard. Edgar, the strange map in hand, exited the passenger side making sure the undone belt of his tan trench coat didn't catch in the slamming door.

"It's a few hours. Fill up a few jerry cans in the bed and we can make it there easily before sunset," Edgar said, enunciating his words through his lipless mouth, teeth chattering with each hard syllable.

"We just leave the strange woman we found in the desert sleeping in my house? Alone?"

"She's stranger than you think."

"What?" Nate asked, turning around and looking at Edgar's emotionless face. "Whatever. Look, it's late enough in the day. We have a nice dinner, relax, and I'll call work and we can go in the morning. I've had enough of running around in the dark. I'll go when the sun is shining and there aren't any monsters jumping out of the dark."

"Night-time is the best time for monsters to jump out of the dark! Isn't that what we're looking for?" Edgar looked over, his eyes threatening to pop out of their exposed sockets.

"I sure as hell hope not," Nate said, unlocking the front door to his house with his dangling keychain. His Miata key was still hanging on it, and it again struck him that he wasn't going to see that car again. More than that, though, he wasn't going to see Brooke anymore, save possibly in a courtroom. She hadn't called. She hadn't demanded an apology or given one. With every passing moment, the loss of her felt increasingly permanent.

"I believe," an unfamiliar, aged yet authoritative voice said, "that you are holding something that belongs to me."

Nate turned. For a moment he thought his eyes must be betraying him, that somehow all this sorrow, this fear and insanity had crossed some wires in his brain, synapses jumping from neuron to neuron in patterns that couldn't possibly be accurately displaying what was happening.

A man stepped out of an ornately jewelled chamber, four boys kneeling beneath the long poles extending from the front and back. The man was in full Pope's regalia, strange metal helmet with a cross atop it instead of the normal white-peaked mitre or skullcap, white robes, long, bladed crooked staff in his hands. The man and his strange vehicle stood where they had just passed moments before. It was him. It was the Pope, standing right in front of Nate. Stranger still, the four boys, each looking like one-winged angels, took to the air holding aloft the embellished boxed cab. It took a moment to realize that there were four robed figures, standing behind the Pope, and even though easily recognizable, Nate couldn't comprehend who they were.

"Kneel before me," the Pope said, "and present to me the ecumenical cartogram." His voice was commanding, so much so that Nate wondered if he had the willpower to deny him. Nate stood in silence, staring, dumbfounded, before finally turning to Edgar.

"I thought this was supposed to be the good Pope," he whispered.

"There is no good Pope," Edgar whispered back. There was a pause as they looked at each other, almost as if both parties needed a moment to understand the other.

"Run for it!" Edgar suddenly yelled, breaking Nate from his trance. Nate looked over, but Edgar was already around the side of the house. Nate jolted into action, bolting for the opposite side, hoping to meet up with Edgar around back.

"Agnus Dei!" the Pope yelled, fury overwhelmed his calm demeanour. "Retrieve that artefact!"

"Achtung!" the Agnus Dei of Hitler barked, cross stamped deep into the waxy complexion of his forehead, "Schnell! Schnell!"

Nate raced around the corner, and above his head the corner of his house exploded, showering splinters and old nails down on Nate as it appeared to have been hit by what must have been a cannonball. Nate covered his head from the dust and dry wood and quickly jutted his head out from the corner to see what they were shooting at him.

They weren't shooting cannonballs at him. It was a fist. Then he noticed Elvis.

One of the robed men was undoubtedly Elvis. Not an impersonator, not the youthful Elvis of the surfing films and Ed Sullivan. It was old, fat Elvis, cross stamped into his forehead like the others. Worse still, his arm had stretched out fifteen, maybe twenty feet, with bulbous waxy growths and swirls, holes and tendrils, making a gurgling noise as it retracted and reshaped itself.

"Holy fuck!" Nate said uncontrollably.

"Blasphemer!" another of the Agnus Die hollered in a distinctly Bostonian accent. Of course, Nate surmised almost without comprehending that it was JFK. Nate ducked behind the corner of the house as the Elvis creature again thrust out his hand, long talon-like fingernails extending from his widespread fingers, slamming against the house and shaking the dust from the shingles above.

"Split up," the Agnus Dei of Michael Jackson said as loud as his soft, effeminate voice could muster, "corner him!" He lifted a leg and swivelled before running off around the far side of the house.

Nate rounded the corner and saw the open desert in front of him. Empty, open space with nowhere to hide. Nate couldn't wrap his mind around what exactly was happening. Long, tendrilous limbs heaving towards him from the bodies of dead celebrities, and the Pope, his flying chair hovering overhead. It wasn't an option to just run out into the open. He looked and saw that Edgar was running behind Stan's house, dodging between Stan's well-maintained desert trees. Nate ran after him, but as soon as he got to the fence, he got hit by a truck. At least that's how it felt.

Nate sucked in breaths of air, wheezing and gasping, laying flat on his back on the desert floor. Blurry-eyed, he looked up. Standing at his feet was John F. Kennedy Jr., black robed and angry, translucent arm recoiled and fist the size of a football.

"Just as easy to take the map off of your dead body," he said through gritted teeth.

Blam!

JFK's head exploded. Edgar stood behind him, trail of smoke rising from his pistol. If Edgar had been capable of smiling, he would have.

"Guess that makes me Lee Harvey Oswald," Edgar said, grabbing Nate by his collar. "Grab your pink pillbox hat and let's go!"

Nate hopped the fence, still gasping from getting the wind knocked out of him. "What... what are those things?" he croaked.

"Agnus Dei. Wax golems with hijacked human souls. They're protected from God, so God has no power to take them to the afterlife. Religious complex uses them as slaves. Poor bastards."

Over another fence and through a yard, an abandoned house that was boarded up provided a bit of cover for them. "Shit, Edgar, what the fuck are we going to do? He's the Pope! He's the motherfucking Pope for Christ's sake!"

"Ah, you've seen one Pope, you've seen them all," Edgar said, peeking around the corner. He quickly let fly two shots in quick succession.

Blam! Blam!

Splortch! The bullet ripped through Michael Jackson's robe and his pale waxy flesh, throwing him backwards. Hitler and Elvis raced down through Stan's yard, heading for the barnwood fence separating his house from the abandoned one.

Blam! Blam! Click.

"You want me to distract them while you reload? I could run across the street or something."

"No point," Edgar said, "no more bullets."

"What! Why the fuck don't you have any more bullets?"

"Sure Nate, why don't you just use the gun you brought, then."

"Fine," Nate said, seconds draining away, adrenaline racing through his veins, "okay, let's try to split them up, and take them on one at a time."

"Agnus Dei? It'd take ten of us to defend ourselves against one of them, and even then, they just ooze through your fingers. I got lucky with that president, hitting him in the seal. No, we're entirely fucked."

"If we just have to remove the seal, we can..."

"Hunka hunka burning love!" Edgar yelled, turning and racing back around the house. Like a snake's strike, Elvis' arm thrust out, wrapping around Nate's neck in its tendrils of waxy flesh.

Edgar rounded the corner, and in front of him, powerful, more menacing than Elvis, was Adolf Hitler, the cross stamped in his forehead aligning perfectly with his small brush moustache.

"Uh, hey Adolf," Edgar said, conversationally stopping and pulling a cigarette out of the pocket of his trench coat, "you know, I'm not German, but uh... I've always liked a good bratwurst."

"Nicht mehr, mein freund," the Agnus Dei of Hitler said, approaching.

With one swift motion, Edgar pulled out the patented 'Bless Me Jesus' aerosol spray, last of his reserves, from a hidden pocket at the back of his trench coat. With a lighter in his other hand, he created an impromptu flamethrower in Hitler's face. "I'm half Polish, you asshole!" he yelled, Hitler recoiling as his face started melting into waxy drips down his forehead, stalactites of wax drooping off of his eyebrows and the end of his nose. Hitler stumbled backwards, and Edgar advanced, ready to finish the job.

"Leave Hitler alone!" Elvis yelled, thrusting out his other arm with a hollow burbling noise and catching Edgar around the foot with a slapping sound, pulling Edgar's feet out from beneath him, 'Bless Me Jesus' spray slipping from his grasp. "Thank you... thank you very much," Elvis said.

Nate struggled for breath, dangling by the neck and Elvis' tentacle-like limb constricted tighter and tighter. He breathed in quickly through his nose, the scent of burnt candles filling his nasal cavity as he hung.

Elvis stopped, stood glassy eyed as three red prongs, fire spilling from the melted wax inside of the robes, thrust through his chest. The limbs relaxed and both Nate and Edgar were released, Nate falling to the ground. Both sets of eyes trapped on the sight of Elvis' melting face, flames wicking up through his robes. The sizzling of the robes were drowned out by the most infernal laughter, deep and deafening.

Nate first registered the decidedly red skin, the horns coming from the forehead and the flaming pitchfork, yanked from the puddle of flaming wax and robes in front of him. He saw the black overalls, the overt manliness. Then he realized who it was.

"Stan?"

"Satan, actually. I guess the whole Stan thing is pretty much moot at this point."

"Satan... like..."

"Yeah," Satan said offhandedly, "I'm the devil. Oh, sorry about the whole fucking your wife thing. Screwing people over is kinda my thing. You know, temptation and all that. Forbidden fruit."

"So... you saved us?"

"I guess so," Satan said, looking up into the sky, seeing the Sedia Gestatoria carried by the four single-winged cherubs high into the sky, "really, I just like fucking with the Pope. What a dick."

"Well," Edgar said, looking at Nate and brushing the dust off of himself, "looks like you really do have a neighbour from Hell."

26

"Well paint me green and call me a cucumber!" Mr. Leone said, looking at ink-jet printed article in front of him. "Flying Popemobiles! Wax Elvis! Nate! Pace yourself for Christ's sake!"

Nate had come in early the next morning. After fighting wax monsters, and being saved by Satan himself, he had been in shock. He'd locked himself in his bedroom for the rest of that evening, sitting and staring at the ceiling.

Everything was different. Everything was strange and unbelievable and bizarre. He had wondered if he was having a mental breakdown, if in reality he was strapped up and laying in some padded room somewhere, imagining the man with no face and hairy monsters in the dark. Maybe it was Brooke cheating on him. It had snapped his brain, he'd thought, but deep down he'd known that wasn't the case. The huge bruise discolouring his entire chest had told him that.

More than anything, he had thought of nothing. He'd sat in his room, not moving for hours. It was almost as if thinking, moving at all, would've triggered some other violent and irrational situation, ghosts might have jumped from the walls, robots would've attacked his house, that sort of thing. So he had done nothing. The entire night. Edgar had knocked at the door, carefully as to not drop the steaming bowl of soup he'd managed to carry up the stairs without spilling. Nate even had thought he'd heard the woman from the desert wake up and go downstairs, but that hadn't mattered. He'd needed the safety of the locked door, the four walls. He'd laid there until he couldn't keep his eyes open any longer, and still only fell hesitantly into a fitful sleep.

But a new day was beginning, and he'd gotten up early, banishing the images of those wax creatures from his mind. He had decided to walk to work. It was a small town, and the ten-minute walk had been refreshing, the cool air of the morning reinvigorating him, bringing him back to the ground after everything in his life had been turned upside down. He'd noticed as soon as he left that Stan's place was empty. The windows and doors were boarded up, and there weren't even any tire tracks left in the dirt. Apparently once his secret was out, Stan had no reason to stay. Nate wondered why he'd lived there at all.

So, at work in the morning, he did what he always did. He wrote. His fingers typed rapidly, trying to recapture every fading moment before it was lost to his brain, suppressing the horrible memories. He exposed the Pope, although the Pope had done very little besides intimidating him and then fleeing. He also strategically left out Satan. He'd do a follow-up article, maybe when the paranoia waned, but for now revealing that his next door neighbour was the Devil was too much. Too much even for the Real World Monitor.

"I once did an article on the Pope," Mr. Leone continued, running his tongue over his lower gums as if trying to remove something wedged in there, "but of course, that wasn't this Pope. He wasn't even a real Pope. He was Grover Cleveland. Of course, he's a vampire now. That's how come he was still alive. Or dead, kind of. Fucking undead." Mr. Leone stood upright, taking the pressure off the filing cabinet that had become his habitual leaning post. "You'd think they'd realize he was a vampire. I mean, they're Catholics!" he said, nudging the back of Nate's chair with his knee. "Catholics, right?"

"Har har har," Hardy laughed from his desk.

"Pope's a saint!" Mike Rant yelled over from his desk. "Anyone who says otherwise is nothing but a godless communist."

"I'm almost done, Mr. Leone," Nate said, realizing that Mr. Leone had already started lumbering off to his office and wouldn't want to be disturbed, "I'm almost done my revisions on the article. I've got to get home. The Pope was after a map that my buddy has, and I have to figure out what to do with it."

"The Pope is after your buddy? Wait... Is it the guy without a face?" he called back, his reporters' instinct kicking in. "Oh Nate, you have got to get photos for me. I mean, that guy is gold. No photo manipulating, no clay models, just a real guy with no face. He could become the poster boy for the Real World Monitor."

"I don't think he'd go for it, Mr. Leone."

"Well, you go and protect yourself from the Pope. We wouldn't want him to baptize you or anything! Ha ha ha!"

Nate hit control P on his computer, and waited for the final draft to be spat out of the machine before shutting down his computer, dropping the papers in the letter box outside of Mr. Leone's office, and walking out on the street in time to see the brown pickup truck screeching to a halt in front of the building.

"Nate," Edgar called over the passenger seat and through the open window. The pale, red-haired woman was sitting beside him, looking around with an amused look upon her delicate features. "Get in. We got stuff to do."

"Why did you bring her?" Nate said, hinges of the passenger's side door groaning as he opened and closed it.

"She was getting bored. Or so I thought. She doesn't talk much."

"Yeah, I noticed. She looks better." Nate noticed that she was wearing an emerald green Hervé Leger dress. It was obviously Brooke's dress, which Edgar must've pulled out of one of the leftover boxes still cluttering the house. It looked strange on her, as if her features needed nothing so decorative. Nate himself was only wearing a pale blue sports shirt with a grey cardigan, while Edgar was wearing his stained dress shirt and black tie beneath the tan trench coat. The pale woman seemed too vibrant between the two of them, too alive, while Nate was felt more jaded and bitter about his life than ever.

"Take a look at her eyes."

The woman turned and looked at Nate. She understood what he had said, kept her eyes opened wide. Nate looked deeply into her eyes. They were aniridic, the pupil huge, far larger than a normal pupil, or even a normal iris. The blackness covered nearly all of her open eye, leaving just the tiniest patches of whiteness at the corners of her eyes. Nate lost himself for a moment, so close to this woman, looking at her beautiful face. He wondered how he'd missed her strange eyes, although upon reflection he'd first seen her in the darkness of the desert night. Since then he wondered if he'd ever actually looked her in the eye, focused more on his own problems than on the person before him. He whispered, mind still miles away. "I never had a chance to ask you your name. What do we call you?"

"English is not my first language," she said, haltingly, "but I have studied it, and I am improving." Her voice was deeper than before, vowels still pronounced slightly incorrectly, although she was getting the hang of it. "I have no name in English."

It was too much, and he turned away, embarrassed that he could get so engulfed in her with his wife gone only days. "Well, we have to call you something."

"You may call me what you wish," she said, turning her gaze to the road ahead of her as Edgar pulled out from the front of the Real World Monitor headquarters and out onto the poorly paved streets.

"Let's call her Zeta," Edgar said, laughing to himself.

"Well," Nate said, "is that okay with you?"

"Adequate," Zeta said. It meant nothing to her. Her people were called something entirely different in her native tongue.

"I filled up the jerry cans with gas. Got a flat of bottled water too, just in case we need it."

Nate looked at Edgar, eyebrows furrowed with confusion. "In case we need it?"

"Alpha and Omega, man," Edgar said, the truck speeding out of the limits of Red Valley, "off to see the wizard."

27

The desert is relentless. It takes from you incessantly, stealing the moisture from you with every breath, burning exposed flesh red and raw, blistering with its touch. It takes and it takes, giving nothing.

Brooke had wandered for days, surviving, barely, thanks to a couple of trickling creeks, or the occasionally muddy puddle. After the shock of the accident wore off, she'd discovered that she had simply walked out into the desert, but when she tried to return to the car, she couldn't find it. Her head still spun from the wound on her forehead, a stinging slit as a reminder to always wear a seatbelt, as well as from dehydration, from heat stroke and the pain of the desert sun beating down upon her.

Her mind raced, reliving days in her life, like the day Nate had surprised her by proposing. They had decided never to get married, as they both figured that marriage was one sure way to kill the love in a relationship, but when he had been on his knee, blue lapis ring, which was all he could afford, in a small velvet box, she couldn't help but say yes.

She'd made mistakes. She admitted that. Sleeping with the neighbour was inexcusable. She still wasn't quite sure why she'd done it. She just felt tempted by those abs, the muscles and manliness, by the confidence and swagger. Tempted by a touch of his hand, maybe, or just a look in his eyes. Maybe it was simply the attention he'd given her when she'd spoken to him over coffees in the early mornings. Pr maybe, years before, saying yes to Nate was the mistake itself. Maybe marriage was the problem. Maybe she was never meant for marriage.

Nate and Brooke had married in Colorado, at the base of La Plata Peak in San Isabel National Park. It was a long hike to even make it to the conifer-laden base, up some steep terrain, but still accessible enough so that their family could make it. There were maybe a dozen people there. Nate's mother was in the country, so she came, although Nate didn't tell his father about it. In fact, he wanted his father to know that he had married, so he sent him an invitation a week later, too late for him to show up. Both of Brooke's parents came, Brooke's brother, Geoffrey, helping her mother up the more challenging sections for someone with limited mobility.

Brooke wore a simple dress, pansies in her hair. Nate had on a tuxedo shirt and tie, Gortex jacket with jeans and hiking boots. Their families might not have understood if anyone else had done this, but knowing Nate and Brooke, it made perfect sense. Out in the light snow of November, they removed their shoes, bare feet on the icy snow, cool and stretching out before them. The temporary marriage commissioner, who was actually a local poet they had befriended, performed the simple ceremony, and even brought his daughter, only three at the time, to hold the two simple gold bands. Lorna was Brooke's maid of honour, still years away from her diagnosis of cancer, and Geoffrey was the best man. Geoffrey's boyfriend, Matt, took photos, and everyone else held hands, encircling the couple as they made their vows.

Cool snow on their feet.

She'd left Nate in such a hurry that she hadn't put on shoes, the only ones in the boxes being high heels. Her bare feet on the scorching earth was excruciating. Then she looked up. Something was out there. Something was present out in the desert. It was a pile of something white, maybe with some red on it, far enough off that she couldn't make it out, but it was not a natural feature. She turned and walked towards it, almost instinctively at this point.

Their life had been good, Nate and Brooke. Life changes, though. Nate's meagre reporter's income wasn't enough, and she had to work. She liked it. She liked getting up in the mornings with a purpose. She liked the tight fitting pant suits and the fierce high heeled shoes and sitting in board meetings. She liked that she'd been headhunted out of the temporary agency and hired on, given responsibilities, responsibilities she'd previously run from. People listened to what she had to say, asked her opinions seriously. People gave her respect, and while maybe that hippie girl with the floral dresses and Birkenstocks was who she had once strived to be, the woman with the slick blond hair and piercing gaze was who she really loved to be. It was like she had been a limbless little tadpole transforming into a frog and crawling out of the swamp. She changed, but that's what life was about, and Nate was supposed to change too. He was supposed to join in on the journey, but he didn't. He was always making up for his lack of self-esteem with schmoozing and trying to act like a big shot, and even with everyone telling him how great he really was, he never believed it. He wore the same tweed jacket with patches on the elbows, and even through all his promotions, she never quite understood why he wanted to be such a big shot news anchorman, when really she suspected he'd have been just as happy working for some crappy paper, reporting car crashes and scam mechanics. But no, he'd been promoted, higher and higher, always striving to impress everyone, while at home, his insecurities came out in the form of dissatisfaction, withdrawing into his books. They'd moved from their small suite up to a high rise, but it just kept feeling emptier and emptier, and Brooke had become increasingly lonely.

That's really when things started falling apart. She was made an executive assistant to a small angry man, and every day he picked away at her, stealing more and more. It was almost as if he expected her to fuck everything up, and she lived up to his negative expectations. She was so worried about the next time he'd yell at her, the next time he'd demean her, cut her with sly insults, that she ended up not actually able to do anything correctly. She was so nervous about what his next horrible attack would be, the next way she would be humiliated, that she neglected her job, missed deadlines, emailed information to all the wrong people, and when confronted with her inability to fulfil the expectations of the job, she couldn't even verbalize what was going on. Her hair started falling out in chunks. She called it alopecia, pretended that it was genetic, but it was stress. An extreme case of telogen effluvium, the doctor had said. The more stress she had, the worse it got. The bald patches were growing more and more noticeable among the other assistants who, for reasons beyond which she could imagine, coveted her position. She lost sleep, she was alone, and Nate was nowhere to be found, emotionally.

The starkness of the desert made travel to the strange white and red lump easier to navigate, and after far too many steps, she finally came close enough to start making out details. It looked like fabric. White fabric. Red spots. Closer still, and her mind was shocked into clarity. It was a body. It was a dead body in a white coat, a bloody white coat. It was ripped apart as if mauled by some large animal. Fingers blackened up to the knuckle on a hand meters away from the rest of the body, chest cavity pulled apart, innards absent. A black briefcase, seeming out of place, laid on the desert floor not far from the body.

She stood and looked at the body. Somehow, the idea of this man's body, unburied, left unprotected against the elements, tugged at her heart.

Loneliness. Maybe that's why she cheated on Nate. The first time, that is. The only time, apart from her recent, incomprehensible illicit affair. Nate's boss was confident, he was powerful and well dressed and obviously took care of himself, sure, but that wasn't why she was attracted to him. While Nate was off schmoozing with other reporters, finding angles to further his career, his boss, she didn't even know who he was at the time, was listening to her. He was listening, and he cared. That was all, but it was a drink of water to a woman dying of thirst. That's all she had ever wanted. She wanted someone to care for her, and he did. Certainly she'd been drinking, and she'd known better than to start with the gin and tonics, but with Nate off on his own, she had figured that it didn't matter. They touched hands under the table, intertwined knees, and she couldn't imagine wanting anything more than to take this man, twenty years her senior at least, and hold his bare skin against hers, fill herself with his scent, his caring and passion. They'd found a small storage closet, and she held him down, rode him, clothes peeled off, until she shuddered and couldn't go any further.

And then Nate. The guilt hit almost immediately. Even as she cleaned herself up, makeup still smeared across her face, Nate found her, and he knew.

He knew and he never let her forget it.

She'd pleaded for forgiveness. She'd begged and promised, and while he said that they could work through it, he hadn't tried. Nothing changed, except the way he looked at her. Like she was disgusting, and sadly, she felt disgusting. That gave way to bitterness, to nitpicking and complaining and making his life miserable. She made him miserable because she was miserable. She made him miserable because she wasn't the girl with the pansies in her hair, barefoot in the middle of a forest. She had become a woman, and Nate… Nate was just Nate. Emotionally selfish Nate, worried about his own career over everything else.

And now Brooke was in the desert, lingering over the remains of someone who, like her, was lost. Holding her breath, she tried to go through his rough pockets, looking for some sustenance, but she knew it was futile. Being this far out in the desert, alone, means he must have been lost, and if he was lost, he'd have likely used up any supplies he'd had.

So she opened the briefcase. It had a strange, plastic seal inside of it, but the stench was still overwhelming. She peeled back the plastic and saw the bloody skin and raw edges. It was a human face.

Brooke threw the briefcase away from her in repulsion. The face falling onto the hot earth, and if she'd had enough moisture within her body to cry, she would've. She looked down at the man, a moment of silence for someone who likely would never be found, never be buried or given a headstone. Someone who was as she would soon be. She held her head in her hands for a moment, pulling away handfuls of hair.

28

Phaedra was having problems of her own, out in the desert, feeling abandoned, forgotten, and now, regretful. Colonel Nine's words ran through her head. No one gets in. Someone tries, someone dies. Now, sitting in the tent, she wondered what had come over her. She attributed it to the desert heat, the voices, haunting her from the desert plains, even her growing suspicion that they spiked her water with LSD, but she knew the real reason. She did it because she was tired of being taken advantage of. It was a simple act of rebellion, her first one since she was a child. She rubbed her fingers together, where she'd touched the oil in the drum. She could still feel the slickness, the petroleum smell permeating her nostrils, and a tingling sensation.

"Why was I forsaken..." the voices cried out.

"So much pain... endless torment..."

And then a sound altogether different. A low hum, a murmur at first and then, unmistakably, an engine.

Phaedra shot of off her bunk, eyes wild with anticipation. Finally, Colonel Nine was bringing a replacement! Finally she was getting out of the desert! Waves of relief washed over her like a cool ocean swell. She smiled, first time in days, and her dry lips cracked at the strain.

And then the realization. The door to the shack had been kicked in. At the last possible moment she lost her mind and broke the one single rule that was given, she'd done it. Worst timing. Worst luck. That was the story of Phaedra's life.

Phaedra grabbed her rifle. She had an image in her head that she'd be standing out in front of the shack like one of the Buckingham Palace guards. She thought about saying that it just collapsed on its own, which actually was quite likely, given the state of the shack. Or, conversely, she could try to quickly restructure the door in the hope that Colonel Nine wouldn't notice the damage.

The rifle felt heavy in her hands, her knees buckled for a moment as she jerkily exited the tent, but she willed herself to keep forcing her way to the shack. The ghostly voices in the distance died down with the increasing sound of the Jeep engine.

But it wasn't a Jeep engine. Phaedra looked up and saw that it was a rusty old pickup truck. It was an intruder.

Phaedra held her rifle at the ready, stood in the doorway of the shack and watched the truck driving across the open landscape. It bumped, weaved around a couple of small shrubs, and minutes later it pulled up at the other side of camp in a cloud of dust.

"Hold it right there!" Phaedra attempted to yell. She realized that she hadn't actually said anything out loud for days, so her voice came out more of a whisper, but pointing the gun at the men getting out of the truck made her point for her.

"Whoa there, buckaroo," Edgar said, "we didn't drive all the way out here to get shot."

Phaedra looked at Edgar but assumed that her eyes were playing tricks on her. She saw Edgar's face, the meaty flesh and gibbous eyes. A third person got out of the truck, a woman in a green dress. "This is military property…" she said, voice still hoarse but at least audible this time, "you have to… you have to leave." Her knee buckled again, but she held herself aloft. It was getting hard to see the three of them. It was as if a bright light were shining in her face, darkening all around the edges.

Nate was feeling exposed. The woman was a soldier, and she had a rifle. There wasn't anything for him to hide behind, so he backed away slightly, hoping that if the bullets started firing he could leap behind the truck, but that didn't seem like it was imminent. Edgar walked right up to the woman, fearlessly. Nate nervously covered his mouth, his fingers running across the long scar on his face. The other wounds were healing nicely, the rat kid scratches almost invisible now under the influence of antibiotics, although the huge gash down the back of his leg would definitely be a visible reminder for the rest of his life.

"You don't look so good, soldier," Edgar said, "you're shaking like a leaf. How long have you been out here?" Zeta wandered up behind Edgar, looking at Phaedra as well. She didn't seem afraid either. Instead, she was just curious. Zeta smiled at her, looking at Phaedra's uniform, and then down at her own green dress.

"A few weeks… maybe a month… I lost track…" Phaedra croaked, eyes darting wildly between the strange faceless man and the two others. She didn't know where to aim her gun. She'd been in the military long enough to have the training, but somehow at that moment, she couldn't recall a moment of it. Terror was rising in her spine, but everything was so blurry, so muddled. "Your face… it's…"

Phaedra buckled again at the knees, the blackness finally engulfing her vision as she crumbled to the dry earth and splintered wood. The gun tumbled to the ground and Edgar, his quick reactions coming in handy, grabbed the woman under the shoulder to ease her down.

"Nate! Where the fuck are you?" Edgar called, only to see Nate standing, sheepishly, by the back of the truck. "Get over here!"

Nate ran over, stepping over the M16 rifle as he came upon the soldier on the ground. "What... what do we do?"

"Get her into the shade," Edgar called decisively, "she's probably got heat stroke, on top of dehydration." Edgar lead the way, dragging Phaedra into the shade of the small shack. He put two fingers up to her wrist but then moved up to her throat. Zeta knelt beside her as well, as if mimicking Edgar's moves, except she lifted up Phaedra's hand. Zeta held it in her own ghostly pale hand, looking at the difference between her skin colour at Phaedra's dark tones. She smiled again, amused by the difference.

Nate stood awkwardly at the door. He had the map in his hand, and this shack was definitely what they were looking for, but it was bare. It was a simple decrepit shack, barely standing, with a barrel in the middle. He looked at the barrel, confused.

Edgar finished checking Phaedra over. "She'll be fine. We should get her to town, cool her off. Get her some water from the back. What's in the barrel?"

"Oil," Nate said. Edgar stood up and looked at the barrel himself.

"Oil?" Edgar said, dipping his finger in, then withdrawing it to smear between his fingers. He gave it a deep smell and held it up to his ear momentarily. "It's consecrated. Strong too. Must be ancient. Good for making oil candles for séances and contacting the dead. That kind of thing. Shit's like catnip to Angles. It's so old it could've been blessed by Moses himself. Wouldn't surprise me. Certainly got the Pope's panties in a knot."

"Get her into the truck," Nate said, "we'll take her back. This is a bust. Consecrated or not, what the hell do we want with a barrel of oil?"

Edgar picked Phaedra up by the shoulders. "Zeta," he said, his voice gurgling, yet somehow softer as he talked to the strange pale woman, "could you grab her feet?"

She picked up her feet without any strain, and they started dragging the unconscious soldier back to the truck. They started stuffing her into the cab when they heard it.

Clang!

Edgar and Zeta looked at each other, momentarily, trying to understand what had happened. Then Edgar raced back to the small shack. "Nate!" he yelled, spotting a pool of oil spilling out from the doorway and between the gaps in the poorly made walls of the shack. Nate came stumbling out of the shack, looking light-headed himself, black oil across his shoes and pant legs, splattered up onto his face, his hands blackened with the consecrated petroleum.

"Something in the oil... it was calling to me..." he said, holding up what looked like a jet black slab of leather slick with greasy black oil. It had grimy yellowed growths on the end, ragged at the top.

Edgar realized what it was only moments before Nate spoke.

"Someone's foot..."

29

"What do we do with the foot?" Nate asked, looking at the wrinkled lump of dried leathery flesh. It bled oil onto a plate on the dining room table in Nate's house. A strange centrepiece, reminiscent of Egyptian mummies displayed at museums with the dry toes curled in tightly. The top was ragged, looking as though it might be torn, and the rest creased and wrinkled. It was charcoal black, discoloured by the petroleum oil it had been mummified in. The noxious scent permeated the room as Edgar, Nate, and Zeta stood around it.

The drive back had been faster, more urgent with Phaedra in such a condition. They'd pulled Phaedra into the house in Red Valley, laid her out on the white B&B Italia sofa. They dripped orange juice into her mouth in an attempt to revive her, laid a cold cloth across her head, laid cold compresses across her chest. She was breathing well, but only occasionally opening her eyes, looking around, perplexed, and then closing them again.

"What do we do with the foot?" Edgar replied incredulously, "I think we have more pertinent concerns. We did just kidnap a soldier."

"We didn't kidnap her!" Nate said, his voice straining. "We rescued her! What were we supposed to do? Leave her out there to the elements? We'd be killing her! We should be taking her to Pronghorn Mesa! We should be taking her to the hospital!"

"I don't know if the military will see this as anything but kidnapping," Edgar said, curiously looking over at the soldier, "and you know the military. They got way too many secrets. Too many right hands not knowing what the left hands are doing." Edgar walked over and looked at Phaedra. "Grover's Mill, Operation Mockingbird, Paul McCartney. Way too many secrets. Way too many agendas."

Zeta reached for the foot, but Nate stopped her hand. "I... uh... I wouldn't do that. Holding it made me feel weird," Nate said. He'd been the only one to touch it so far, and it had given him a tingling sensation when he did. The entire trip back he'd been feeling a strange, prickling feeling, almost like an itch deep down in his bones, a taste in his mouth, soapy almost, floral, that almost overpowered the horrible smell of the oil soaked foot. Apart from that, he actually felt good. His chest didn't ache from the huge bruise across it, and he seemed to be breathing better. The ever-present throbbing from the stitched up wound on the back of his leg dulled too, so much so that he didn't feel it at all. But it wasn't a numbness. Not really. It was more like the pain was gone, replaced with a strangely warm, tingling sensation, and there was also an odd feeling like his senses were heightened. This hadn't been a bonus while they'd been stuck in a hot truck cab with three other people, one who had been in the desert for God knows how long and without access to a shower, and, of course, a mummified foot drenched in crude oil.

There was, though, a slight clarity of thought, a lucidity he hadn't felt for a long time. His mind raced with insights into things, a sense of his own responsibility towards his own life, and even a temporary relief from the sadness of Brooke's departure, maybe only fleeting, but urgently welcomed.

The foot looked ancient and well preserved. Nate had picked it up without thinking, and suddenly the thought of ancient diseases, like the bubonic plague, zipped along the corners of his thoughts and he rapidly deposited the foot back onto the ceramic plate. Zeta looked at him for a moment, a questioning look crossing her alien face at being rebuffed from touching the foot. There were a lot of customs that she didn't understand about the culture, so after a quick nod, a gesture she'd noticed Nate and Edgar do when they came to an understanding, she walked over to Phaedra.

"She looks better," she said, her voice deep.

"I still say we should take her to the damn hospital!"

"You want to put her back into that rust bucket with no air conditioning, be my guest. I'll bring daisies to her funeral," Edgar said. "We wait for darkness. Her temperature is better. She looks pretty beat up. Probably be out for hours."

"Why would the army just abandon her in the desert?" Nate added in. "Is she, like, Black Ops or something?"

"Why would they have her guarding a foot in the middle of the desert?" Edgar said. "Why would they be keeping a foot in a barrel of oil? Why does the American government have plans to convert all of the Walmarts into FEMA prison camps? You think I got all the answers?"

"You have more damn answers than I have!"

"Hey, you all right?"

"What?" Nate asked, almost tongue-tied over the sudden shift in Edgar's demeanour.

"You look different. Like you got a haircut or something."

"No," Nate said, "Nothing's changed. I feel good. Great, really, but that's not the point."

Edgar pulled the linen map out of the inside pocket of his trench coat, "Well, I did notice this, though. Look."

Nate took the map and spread it out on the ottoman, getting down on one knee and flattening out the creases in the coarse linen fabric. The map was darker, as outside the sun was sinking into the horizon. Nate looked at it, Zeta lingering over his shoulder. She had her hand on his shoulder, her body close to his, and he felt her warmth, her breath near his ear. It was intoxicating, but he needed to focus.

The map had changed. The landscapes, the lines changing from the organic dried riverbed and hills to a grid pattern. It wasn't the desert anymore. It was Red Valley, and the symbol, the Chi Rho symbol, the P with the X across its stem, was directly on Nate's house.

"Shit... it... it knows where we are..." Nate stammered, unsure of what he was even trying to say.

"Yeah, looks like the map shows you where the foot is, so that leaves us with a problem. The Pope is after us, probably over this stupid foot. He's got Agnus Dei, probably two left as they usually travel in sets of four, but who knows what else he brought with him. There's all sorts of nasties that he has access to, and we're cowering in a living room with the curtains closed."

"So what do we do with the foot?" Nate asked.

30

Across the street, Beatrice Hetherington was in mourning. She'd battled depression her whole life, sure, but this was different. Her son was dead.

Beatrice, like so many of her neighbours, had grown up in Red Valley. Daughter of the Mayor, back when being the Mayor of Red Valley was a full-time job. He pulled together the commercial downtown district to cater to the constant flow soldiers coming into town for training in desert operations, and supported the construction of the resort, which thrived for thirty years before going bankrupt when the military pulled out. He was also responsible for the library, put it in the books that it would be maintained in perpetuity, and that Beatrice would be the head librarian. He took care of her, and still did from beyond the grave. He bought her a house, bought her a car, made every aspect of her life comfortable. All except one.

Beatrice had never found love. Not really. Beatrice was small, not very attractive, and set in her ways early on in her life. She held the soldiers in disdain, nothing but beefy thugs, bravado-fuelled drunkards at the local bar, sickly pathetic weaklings nursing hangovers at The Lucky. She avoided them, even ones who wandered into her small library looking for Hemmingway or Graham Greene. She'd check out books for them, suspicious whether or not they'd return them before getting shipped off to other God-knows-where. Most often they didn't.

The years passed, her life passed, almost without incident. She had a routine, a set menu for evening meals, Saturday morning indulging with breakfast at the Lucky, chatting with Irma the waitress, before opening the library late, Sunday church meeting followed by weekly house cleaning and a few hours of reading before bed. She'd never left town. She'd never kissed a man. She just lived a quiet, solitary life.

That was before she'd had the dream. That was before Smitheos.

It had been a nondescript evening when she first met him. Beatrice couldn't even tell exactly when the dream was. She'd been walking through a field of flowers, purple and red and yellow, as Beatrice always dreamed in vivid colours. She'd found the man sitting on a stone bench, and although there weren't any gravestones around, Beatrice could tell it was a cemetery. He had wounds on his arms and legs. Burns. When she sat beside him, she saw that he wasn't exactly a man. His features were rat-like, his matted brown hair slicked back to show his sunken red eyes, his elongated face and downturned nose extending into the split philtrum, exposing his long front teeth. His ears were further back on his head, pointed slightly, and he wore only burned rags.

"I am poor," he'd said, "I'm misshapen and worthless. Please, be on your way." Beatrice stood, looking at him, and couldn't leave. Maybe she felt was a kinship with him. Maybe it was because she'd been told too many times how ugly she was, how pitiful and small and worthless. How she'd never amount to anything. For all her father gave her, he could not erase the harsh words of the children at school, could not give her self-esteem, try as he did. She sat with the poor rat man on the stone bench.

The dream returned, not every night, but often. She'd sit, and they'd talk. She talked to her dream friend more than anyone she'd ever talked to in reality. She told him about the cruelty of her peers, her loneliness, her solitude. Then one night, he told her his story.

He said he was from a small village where a cruel and greedy bishop ran the church. He forced the townsfolk to build him a tower, and atop the tower was the most luxurious room anyone had ever seen. He bought expensive rugs, bed frame of gold, and jewelled cups. He then took the strongest of the lads and gave them weapons, enforced heavy taxes on the port, passing ships losing half of their wares for simply docking. This forced the ships away, so to make up the shortfall he had taxed the farmers, taking most of their grain and storing it in his great tower. The village people were starving, growing increasingly angry and rebellious, so he invited the fathers of each family to come to a storage house to carry back with them two sacks of grain. Instead, once the men of the families were inside of the storage house, he locked the doors, burned it to the ground.

That's how Smitheos had gotten his burns.

Now, years later, Beatrice made her way up the creaky stairs in her house. Her two sons were hungry. They, like her, were in mourning over the death of their brother, although today they had been agitated. They had been fighting with each other, running in circles, throwing themselves against the bars of their enclosure.

"Calm down, boys! Jesus!" Beatrice said, "Lord have mercy, what has gotten into you today?" She looked through the bars at the faces of the two rat kids. There was a sadness about them, their eyes sunken and sad, the little downturned mouth of the smallest of her rat kids, now simply the smaller of the two, cutting through her harsh treatment of them, bringing Beatrice's own sorrow to the surface. "I'm sorry, boys. I know you miss your brother. I do too."

But it was more than that. It was more than just missing their brother. There was something in the air that night, something imperceptible to Beatrice, to her entirely human senses.

Smitheos and Beatrice kissed the night he'd told her how he got his burns, both looking young and full of life, but Beatrice hesitated, didn't fully allow herself to love him.

"Are you just a dream," she asked him the next night, walking through a forest so lush and green she could almost taste it, "are you a spirit? Are you alive? Are you... are you dead?"

"I didn't always look like this," Smitheos said, seeming to ignore the question, "I was a regular man. I was never even a father, never the head of a household, but I lived with my brother and his wife and children. He had grown too weak from hunger, so I volunteered to take his place, to get the grain for his family myself. I wasn't even supposed to be there."

"I'm so sorry," she said, looking at his soft features, the thin fur on his brow.

"Thank you," he said, looking into her eyes, "I'm sorry. I don't know what I am. I've been here so long. I've forgotten so much."

They made love that night for the first time, two bodies intertwined in the soft foliage of the forest giving in to their deepest desires. Both attuned to each other, yet awkward in their inexperience.

Her little rat-children were suffering, and as exhausted as she was of the constant scratching on her ceiling, the squeals and shrieks, she knew she was the only one who would ever take care of them, so she made her way down the creaky stairs of the old house. She opened the back door, the heat of the day abating with a cool desert breeze. The chickens in the coop had quieted, nesting for the night. She unlatched the chicken wire fence, then the door to the coop. She looked at her chickens, all lined up on their shelves, each one jerking awake. She had twenty chickens at any given time, so she quickly determined which were the two largest and threw them into the brown burlap sack she kept by the door. This would be their meal for the night. A special meal. In memoriam.

The next night Smitheos had seemed sad, distant. He sat on his bench and didn't take to his feet as he had in previous nights.

"What is the matter?" Beatrice had asked him. She had no experience with men. She didn't know if he was unhappy with her, if he'd gotten what he'd wanted and was done with her. She didn't know if she was just disappointing, like she'd always thought she'd be.

"You don't deserve me," he said, and for a moment she misunderstood, thought that he put himself in such high regard that he deserved someone better than she was. Part of her agreed with him, but then he continued speaking. "I'm not a good man. I've done bad things."

"What do you mean?" she asked, the dreamy sky swirling with purple and blue clouds, mimicking her own inner turmoil.

"After the bishop killed us, killed me, I did some things I shouldn't have."

He explained himself as best as he could. He didn't have the exact words to explain where he was, or what he was, but something was left after his body died. Something continued to exist for him, and maybe not for any of the others locked in that storage house, but part of him lived on. He somehow, some way beyond his own comprehension, concocted a deal with the rats, and on the first night, the night of his own death, the rats came into that tower and ate all the grain. They ate every last piece, gnawed holes in every sack, gnawed through the handles of the shovels and buckets.

In the morning, the bishop was furious and ordered the extermination of every rat in the village. Problem was, there were no rats to be found. Not a single rat anywhere. Guards pulled apart woodpiles, dug into every burrow, but nothing. No rats.

The next night, while the bishop slept, the rats stole into his chambers. They chewed through all his fine carpets, plucked the jewels from all of his goblets and rings, even chewed his mattress until it was nothing but strands of cloth, save for the very spot his body covered. They gnawed through the wood on the chairs, the tables, the bureaus and cabinets. They left nothing of value except the bare golden bed frame.

"And the third night," Smitheos said, "I won't tell you of that night, save that there was blood, and I took this form forever more."

Beatrice stood at the cage doors, her feral offspring scratching at the bars of their cages with their long, yellowed claws, screeching and gibbering to themselves in a fury of frustration.

"Calm down boys, I have something special for you," she said, pulling the chickens out of the burlap sack by their feet. The birds flapped and squawked, refusing to accept their fate.

"Mmm! Yummy chicken for my boys," she said. She unlatched the cage and dangled the chickens for the rat kids to grab. "That's right. You like killing things, don't you?"

Smitheos and Beatrice made love again in that dreamy night, but it was different. Smitheos had bared his soul, and in doing so, his touch was more tangible, his warmth filling her as he held her in her arms. That night, Beatrice became pregnant with her dream child.

The first one was born, not in just a dream but in real life, and only five months since conception. Beatrice hadn't shown, hadn't missed a day at the library. It was a small pink bundle, not exactly human, not exactly of this world. It was a child conceived in the dreams, and it seemed like it was always half there. She still dreamed of Smitheos, spent their nights together under the surreal skies of the dream world, but their child never joined them. Nor did the second, nor the third. On the night of the birth of their third child, Smitheos had seemed extraordinarily sad. Beatrice was celebrating, overjoyed that for once in her life, she was good enough, she was needed, desired, and loved.

After that night, she never dreamed of Smitheos again.

Cage open, the rat kids, her children, leapt from the darkness of their attic room. The eldest, as feral and wild as they'd always been, extended a claw as it bypassed the dangling chicken and accidentally caught Beatrice across the face, cutting her deeply. The two rat children scrambled down the stairs, claws scratching at the hardwood and linoleum until they made it out the back door and out into the cool night.

"You ungrateful little..." she screamed, chickens flapping in fear all around her. "Get back here!"

31

Edgar stood out on the front porch of Nate's house. He held the cigarette between his teeth, lit it, and inhaled deeply. The realization was hitting him that even if he did find Dr. Tarentola, even if he did get his face back, it was too late. Too many days had passed, too long spent in the hospital, too distracted by the mysterious map and finding the mummified foot.

Maybe it was more though. Maybe he was distracted by Nate himself. Maybe, for once, he found someone that he could call a friend. Nate's natural state of confusion, his lack of any frame of reference for what he was undoubtedly in the middle of, and the authenticity of his complete bewilderment gave Edgar a bit of faith in the man. He wasn't a plant, wasn't a spy for the Odd Fellows, wasn't Illuminati or from the St. Nicholas Society of New York. He was just a guy. Just some dupe, some everyday nobody who was blooming into enlightenment. Maybe that's what he saw in him. Promise.

Edgar exhaled a thick puff of smoke. It seeped out of his gaping cheekless mouth, stung his nearly lidless eyes. He wasn't going to get cheeks. Not his cheeks. He always thought that at the end of things his life would be returned to normal, but there was never an end to things. It was always being hunted, always stumbling upon something that he wasn't supposed to know. Some secret that he couldn't share in fear that the person he confided in would either be targeted by the conspiracy, or would be part of the conspiracy itself. He thought that one day he would be vindicated, returned whole. Now, it seemed, he would never be whole again. He was the faceless man now, he was terrifying, but he had a job to do.

His train of thought was stopped short by screeching yelps, the padded footfalls racing towards him. He recognized the shrieks of the rat kids. He turned and fumbled to open the door, succeeding in opening it, but it was too late to close it. The rat kid slammed into the door, bursting it open and throwing Edgar sprawling into the living room. Edgar grunted as his body flopped to the floor.

"Fuck!" Nate managed to yell, picking up the closest thing to him that he could imagine as a weapon, which turned out to be Brooke's Eternity Lamp. He held it firmly in both hands, wielding it like a staff. He stepped forward, bulb bright and pointed towards the small rat kid that had overtaken its larger brother. "Get! Get the fuck out of my house!"

The small rat kid lurched back from the light, over the back of the white sofa and onto Phaedra's chest. She jolted into consciousness, face to face with the malformed creature, yellow incisors within snapping distance as she lay prone beneath the rat-like thing.

"Gah!" she yelled, surprising both herself and the rat kid.

"Protect the foot!" Edgar yelled, dragging himself up off of the ground.

"Jesus!" Phaedra yelled, scrambling to shove the rat kid off of her chest. Suddenly, Edgar was there, holding his Beretta to the face of the rat kid, pushing it forcefully into the creature's forehead.

"I don't know if you understand me, but you understand this. Now get the Hell out of this house," he grunted through gritted teeth. But the small vermin-like creature, reflexes beyond human, swatted the gun from Edgar's hand, raking its claws through his exposed palm in the process. Edgar jerked his hand back in pain.

"The gun was empty anyway!" he spat out, and before he could react further, the rat kid leapt upon him, knocking him to the floor again. Phaedra shot up off of the sofa and reached around for her rifle. It wasn't there. Phaedra had no idea where she was, but she instantly felt the naked sensation of not having her weapon in her hands.

Soldier instincts kicking in, she quickly noted all possible threats before choosing her course of action. There was a man with terrible facial wounds being attacked by some unknown creature. The second of these strange, rat-like creatures had advanced upon the man with the lamp, but he seemed to be holding his own for the moment. The other, the one that was just on top of her, it was now on top of the faceless man, clawing at his chest mercilessly. Phaedra hesitated for only a moment longer.

The claws were digging into Edgar's chest, worse with every swipe. He tried to push the rat kid off of him but its hind claws were holding firm onto his body. His shirt was in tatters, bloody and shredded, and it was all he could do to keep his neck protected.

"Flying forearm smash!" Edgar heard, before seeing Phaedra leap, a strange green glow about her, smashing the rat-kid across the face and shoulder with her forearm. Phaedra tumbled off of the thing and rolled back to her feet. Edgar rolled over, started crawling for safety behind the chaise.

Nate was having his own problems. The smaller of the two rat kids had retreated when he waved the bright end of the expensive standing lamp in its face, but this bigger one, more vicious looking than the other, was unafraid of the bright light. He waved the lamp back and forth, cursing the short power cord which limited his movements. Zeta was behind him, and she looked on, seemingly unaware of the threats before her.

Suddenly, Zeta put her hand on Nate's shoulder, stepped towards the large rat kid. It stopped trying to attack Nate, and stood, looking at her. She got closer, so close that the creature could sniff her face. Nate stood there, dumbfounded, wondering what she was doing.

In an instant everything changed. The rat kid bared its teeth, and lashed out, ripping its claws across Zeta's delicate features. Then it seemed to hesitate. Zeta was bleeding, but it wasn't red blood at all. It was a deep purple liquid, like a thick syrupy grape juice, except that it gave off a smell like bleach and honey. She put her hand up to her face, pulling it away to see the blueish-red blood on her fingertips.

Then she opened her mouth. Her voice was in the lower range normally, almost sultry, but the sound that started emanating from her mouth at that moment was anything but feminine. Anything but human. It started as a low rumble, so deep as to barely register on the scale of human hearing, but loud and growing louder still. The floor started vibrating, and Nate put his hands up to his ears in an impotent act of trying to shield himself. The sound, though, came up through his body, so loud that it was hard to think. Edgar was on the floor holding his own ears, and Phaedra, who was still standing to defend herself from the small rat kid, was struggling to stay on her feet, her stance stiff and her fists were clenched, but her features were blurred from the light emanating from her skeleton. She was glowing so brightly that each of her bones were fully visible, tingeing everything in green light, even in the bright light of the living room.

The rat kids writhed on the ground, unwilling to give up their prey, but the deep sound wracked through their bodies, made breathing difficult, until the larger of the two, purple blood still on its claws, turned and raced out of Nate's house, the smaller one following close behind.

Blood was flowing from Nate's nose, and Phaedra, her skeleton still glowing brightly beneath her flesh and organs, had fallen to her knees beneath the encompassing thunder of Zeta's voice. Zeta didn't stop. Nate felt his teeth shaking in his gums, his bones grinding together. The front window of the house shattered, leaves fell off the Bird of Paradise, and in the kitchen the cupboard doors shook open, shattering plates falling onto the faded linoleum.

"Zeta," Edgar yelled, chest bloodied, shirt in ribbons, "they're gone. Calm." Zeta exhaled deeply, her voice waning into silence. For a moment, no one said a word. It was quiet in the house.

"God, my head," Phaedra mumbled.

"Thought we were going to have a brown note moment there for a second," Edgar grunted.

"What the hell was that?" Nate said, sitting up on the floor, wiping the blood away from his nose onto his sleeve. "How... how did she do that?"

"Nate, I was trying to be gentle with you, but I guess the time for that is over," Edgar said, looking around the living room at the devastation that Zeta's deep toned scream had caused. "Haven't you wondered about her eyes? That accent that doesn't seem to be from anywhere?"

"I thought maybe it was one of those African languages. You know, the one with the clicks."

"Do you think people from Africa have purple blood and the scream at a million decibels? Nate, Zeta isn't from Africa, brother. She's an alien."

"Alien? Like, from outer space? You have got to be shitting me."

"Look at my face," Edgar said, leaning in close to Nate, red grisly flesh and exposed cartilage, "does it look like I'm shitting you?"

Zeta, sensing the threat was gone, turned her attention back to the foot.

"Look, guys," Phaedra said from across the room, "I don't know you from Adam, and I don't know how I got here or what the fuck is going on, but I have to get back to my post."

"Yeah," Edgar said, "about that. We thought you were going to die out there, so we brought you with us."

"You do realize," Phaedra said, her glowing skeleton faded to the point where it couldn't be seen in normal light, "that I had lots of food and water in the tent? I had ice packs and fans?"

Edgar shot a look over to Nate, who was still staring in disbelief at nothing in general. The fact that he'd been harbouring an extraterrestrial had apparently short-circuited his brain.

"Uh... no, we didn't look in the tent," Edgar admitted.

"I shouldn't be around people! I'm not safe!"

"What, the glowing skeleton? Have you looked at me? Do you think I'm worried that your skeleton is glowing? That's the most normal thing I've come across in weeks."

"I'm radioactive! I can't be around anyone!"

"Yeah, because we're so health conscious," Edgar said. The look on Nate's face easily conveyed that he was not in agreement.

Behind Edgar, and behind Nate, Zeta extended a single finger, only slightly and delicately touching the black, mummified foot. She held her finger there, and, slowly at first, the purple scrapes across her face started closing up, meshing together and pulling tightly, until moments later there was no evidence that she'd been wounded at all except for the purple blood that still stained her face and hands.

"Zeta," Nate said, turning around, "your face... it's... it's fine."

"Alien physiology," Edgar said, "nanites, orgone energy healing. Nothing to concern yourself with."

"It's more than fine," Nate said, wiping away the blood streaks from her face, exposing the perfect porcelain skin, her dark alien eyes. "It's perfect."

"I'm sorry for the damage," Zeta said, her voice now raspy and dry, "I was hurt, and I reacted... poorly." Zeta put her hands onto Nate's face, running her fingers across his soft, smooth skin.

"Ah, young love," Edgar said, his gurgling voice distracting Nate, forcing him to pull away from Zeta in embarrassment. "Too bad he's married."

"Hm," Phaedra said, caught off guard, "doesn't look married to me."

"Hey, see that foot over there?"

"That black thing on the table? Yeah?"

"We stole it from your base," Edgar said, a laugh erupting from his skeletal face.

32

Brooke slumped down on the dark desert floor, legs no longer able to carry her. It was night, and she'd been walking all day. Walking for days, sipping water from tiny puddles in the rocks, licking dew off of the manzanita shrubs, chewing on chia sage for sustenance, once finding a prickly pear cactus to take both liquid and nourishment from. She hadn't seen any signs of civilization, save the dismembered body of the doctor. She wouldn't last one more day. She doubted if she would last the night. The desert had broken her. Her feet were red and swollen, her skin red and peeling, and her hair had large bare patches in it from her alopecia.

She lay where she had crumpled, face down, on her knees. Ants climbed up on her arms and legs and started biting. She had fallen on an anthill, so she forced herself, gathering the last remnants of strength from her aching muscles, up to her feet. She shuffled on into the darkness. For all she knew, she could've been walking in circles. It didn't matter to her anymore. She was a dead woman.

But the question in her mind now, in her final moments, was that if she were to do it over again, would she have done anything differently? Would she have been a different person had she been given the chance? She thought for a moment and decided she absolutely would have done things differently.

She would've evolved again. She would've left Nate earlier. Maybe she wouldn't have married him in the first place. Regardless, he changed her, inadvertently taken her identity, bit by bit, and she saw it happening and did nothing. She would've left the city instead of getting used to ten dollar lattes and hundred dollar bottles of wine. She would've moved North, lived in the forests. Far, far away from the desert. She would've started a bed and breakfast, or even just found a cabin deep in the woods and lived off of the land. She would've shed the Marc Jacob dresses, replaced them with flannel shirts. Sure, maybe she was romanticizing living off of the land, maybe would've hated every moment of it, maybe even worse than she hated the desert, but that's where her mind went. Clean, clear rivers, wildflowers, solitude, and freedom from Nate. She knew she shouldn't place all the blame on him. She'd done as much damage as he did, probably more, but changing and growing was integral to her being, and he wanted things just to always follow his plan. She wanted to be a hippie again, and a lumberjack, and a fashion maven, and whatever else she felt like. She wanted to grow her hair long, then cut it back, braid it one day, straighten it the next. That was who she was, and pin-holing herself into a job, into an identity, was stifling. Maybe that's why she sabotaged her marriage.

Sabotaged her marriage. The words took the breath from her. The realization stinging more than her sunburn.

The desert ants behind her, she kept shuffling on, half asleep, half deranged. She was lost in thought so much so that she failed to notice the silhouettes off in the distance. Five, maybe six figures, about the size of bears, although hard to tell from a distance. Brooke just wandered on, not noticing them. They noticed her, though.

She made a list of everyone she would have wanted to apologize to. Her mother and father, for disappointing them, for not visiting, not calling often enough. She'd apologize for being a rebellious teenager, smoking pot in the basement. They must have noticed her glassy eyes and the unmistakable smell of burning cannabis. She would apologize for not visiting when her mother had her hip replacement, sent a measly floral arrangement instead of sitting by her bed.

She'd apologize to her brother for their childhood spats, for stealing from his piggy bank to buy beer. She'd apologize for moving away and being distant just as he was coming into his own and needed advice from a sister. Never talking to him about love. Never helping him tell their parents about his boyfriend, be there to support him through their adjustment, their refusal to believe that it was more than just a phase.

She would not apologize to Nate. She did him wrong, there was no doubt about that. She should've been straightforward with him, instead of trying to fulfil her emotional needs through physical encounters. She admitted that. She owned it, but she wouldn't apologize. No, she wouldn't, because he would never own his half of the problem, so it would be wasted breath anyway.

The large creatures loped closer and closer to Brooke, who walked on obliviously. Smelling the ground behind her, footprints in the dry earth, they followed along, surprisingly silent for such large creatures. They approached cautiously. They knew that these upright creatures were dangerous, had weapons. They knew to take their prey by surprise.

The man in the desert. The doctor, torn apart. Brooke was thinking of him, and the briefcase. She wondered if the severed face in the briefcase had belonged to the faceless man, the man who had saved them the night Nate was attacked.

She'd lived in desert cities, but never out in the desert, and she didn't know the dangers. She didn't know where to check for scorpions, which kinds of snakes were safe and which were venomous. She had no idea of the creatures, coyotes or rat kids, cougars or chupacabra. She was a foreigner in her own country.

She stumbled over a small shrub. She hadn't been looking where she was going. She wasn't thinking about much now. Simply moving, simply continuing on, as stopping would mean death, and she wasn't ready to die. Close, but not yet.

So when she turned and saw the lunging beast, spines down its back rigid and upright, dog-like head with its cavernous mouth wide, horrible razor-edged teeth thrusting at her vulnerable throat, she screamed, but her voice was too weak and raspy from the dry desert air to even be audible.

33

Umba was tired. Umba was confused and frustrated and filled with guilt. He'd dragged his clan into the desert, from the lush forests, traveling for days, weeks. They'd traveled at night, eight of them in total, when it was coolest. The Bigfoot are not desert creatures, with their long fur and thick, heavy set bodies. Also, night was best for crossing freeways, passing by small camps, stumbling upon locals who no one would ever believe anyway. They'd ransack the campsites, stealing food and water, while the locals would run in fear. He'd pushed his clan, and they respected him. After all these years, he'd gained that respect.

Years earlier, too many to tell, back when he was still courting Cinnamon, the clan hadn't accepted him. He'd tried to share in with the meals, only to be driven away by the strongest warriors, the elders commanding them with looks and simple grunts. In those days he had known well enough to run back to his ramshackle cabin. He was no match for their incredible strength, but he had always returned. Slowly, he began sitting with them. They had seen that he could build fires, so Umba was put in charge of keeping a fire going, teaching the others how to make fire from available materials. Umba hadn't thought that the smoke and light might attract anyone. He had been wrong.

There had been a logging camp, far enough for safety, but not far enough. A couple of the guys had seen the fire and smoke, thought they'd go investigate. They'd hacked through the woods, trampled the saplings and scared off the wildlife. The noise had given the clan enough warning to hide in the foliage of the forest, but not much more.

There'd been three of them, thick puffy jackets, heavy hiking boots and backpacks. One had brought a rifle, carrying it across his back. They'd stomped in, seeing the logs set up for sitting on, seeing the fire embers burning down, the primitive tools. They'd called out a few times into the forest, but the clan had stayed still, their hot breath visible only to themselves in the cool waning light of the evening.

But then one man had started walking to the edge of camp, to where a pack of the Bigfoot had been hiding. Rifle drawn, he had called out again. It'd shocked Umba that the man hadn't seen any of the clan, as likely one of them could have reached out and touched him. Tension rising in the group, something was going to happen. Umba had seen an attack was imminent. He'd known that even if they managed to get away unhurt, maybe one of them grabbing the gun away from the foolish logger, then they might have ended up killing one of them, or worse yet, let them escape to tell the world about their lives there. Either way, it would be a disaster for the clan. It would have been what they had always feared.

"Hey!" Umba had yelled, running out of the bush. He was still a young man then, his long beard still brown instead of grey, and he wore furs over his shoulders to keep warm in the cool climate. "You sons-a-bitches get away from my camp!"

"Shit!" the rifleman had yelled, turning his gun on Umba. Collectively the clan had gasped, muscles tensed, ready for battle. "You scared the fuck out of me! What are you doing out here?"

"Who sentcha?" Umba had yelled, wild eyed with fear. "You government men? You leave me alone!"

"He's a fucking lunatic," the other logger had said, spitting on the ground, "leave him alone."

"Yeah," the rifleman had replied, lowering his gun, "yeah, you just watch out for yourself out here, you old coot. There's weird shit in this forest."

They had turned and walked away, and the clan, still in hiding, had seen Umba stand in front of the man with the weapon for them, and even though they didn't understand his words, they had realized that he'd sent them away, protected the clan. After that, Umba sat with them at the fires, and as the older Bigfoot died off, the younger ones growing into massive adults, Umba had somehow become one of the elders, respected, revered.

But bringing them out into the desert had been a mistake. Umba cursed himself for his own foolishness, his own stupidity. Maybe he was growing older, dementia setting in, but deep within him, deep in his bones, he felt something. He felt something drawing him deeper into the desert.

He could've come alone. He didn't have to bring Cinnamon, or the six warriors. He could've come alone, walking in the daylight, maybe even hitchhiking as he used to back when he was young back before he had his first car. But Red Valley had called him, brought him back.

He heard the screeching and skittering claws well before he saw anything, but Cinnamon was already alert. She'd heard something else, something that he couldn't. Maybe her range of hearing was better than his, or then again, he was an old man, and maybe it was just age and deafness. The screeching, gibbering voices, though. That was unmistakable.

The warriors got into position, spreading out to flank whatever was approaching. They were unaccustomed to the open landscape, sparse trees and hiding places, yet they found some small pinyon pine, ragged rabbitbrush and outcropping rocks to hide behind.

The two things came into their territory, stopped, and smelled the air. Umba was certain that their scent was unmistakable. Still, it was too late. The largest of Bigfoot warriors leapt out, caught the thing by surprise and grabbed it around the neck. It screeched and yelped in the huge hairy monster's grasp. The second one scampered off, whimpering, into the darkness of the desert night.

It was just a child, they thought, holding the rat kid up by the throat, its limbs dangling and clawing ineffectually.

"What is it?" Umba called, running out from his own hiding spot. It was dark, but they were all used to darkness, night hunting in the forest. Umba looked at the thing, rat-like, claws, sunken eyes and strange, malformed head. The thing had blood on it, not its own, but something else as well. "Hold it still!"

Umba grabbed its dangling arm, held its clawed hand close to his face and sniffed deeply. His body shivered and he was instantly covered in goosebumps. "It's blood... not normal blood though..." he said, blinking rapidly, "and I think I know this scent... I don't know how..."

"Grrrrr..." Cinnamon growled, baring her teeth at the rat kid.

The rest of the warriors circled the four of them, marching sluggishly in a wide perimeter, scouring the darkness for the other rat-like child, but to no avail. It had gone, and there was nothing else that could be considered a threat. Tense moments passed, and finally Cinnamon released the rat kid, tossing it out into the desert where it scampered away, its back arched, looking behind it to see if they were following. It sniffed the ground and ran off in search of its sibling.

"We need to continue," Umba said, "we need to move on. We're so close."

34

"You broke into a military outpost and stole a top secret military... foot!?!" Phaedra yelled, shocked that the situation had moved far, far beyond just removing her from her post. Now she was in the middle of a huge clusterfuck. There'd likely be a government inquiry, a court martial, possibly prison time. She couldn't wrap her brain around how she could explain this to Colonel Nine, how she could convince him she hadn't been complicit in the theft.

"Well, to be honest," Edgar said, clasping another cigarette between his teeth and pausing to light it, "it was more of a military shack, and it wasn't that difficult."

"Whatever! This is the military we're talking about! These guys have the government on their side! You think they're just going to accept this? You think they're just going to shrug their shoulders and say 'well, I guess even though we hid it in the middle of the desert and had a full-time guard, it's gone now. You think that's plausible?"

"You have to understand," Nate said, "we were trying to save your life. The foot was just... I don't know... I just grabbed it. I can't imagine that the military has much interest in a human foot. Seriously, maybe it's, like, a mummy foot or something, but then they should have put it into a museum, not a barrel of oil."

"Who said they put it in there. Maybe it came out of the ground that way," Edgar chimed in, "maybe they sucked it out of the ground with the oil. You don't know."

"You're not helping!" Nate yelled, louder than he had intended.

"The military is different. They tell you what to do, and you don't ask. I don't know why they had a foot in a barrel. I don't know why no one came for me, or why I was hearing shit. It's just..." Phaedra said, her voice trailing off, the fight leaving her with all of the confusion. "Is it really just a foot? That's all that was there?"

"Just a foot," Nate said, relaxing a little. Phaedra walked over to the foot. It still sat on the plate in a puddle of oil. It was warped, nails ragged, flesh blackened and leathery.

"So," Edgar said, exhaling a puff of smoke through his yellowed teeth, "tell us more about what you heard."

Phaedra hesitated, squinting her eyes at the faceless man. "Just voices, mostly. Like, when it got real, real quiet, the whispers would start, and it was like they got louder and louder. They were calling for help, or swearing at me, threatening me. I think the heat was getting to me."

"Consecrated oil," Edgar grumbled, "makes sense."

Nate righted an overturned dining room chair and sat on it, light shining down on the foot from the simple overhanging light fixture his father had installed. "What the fuck is with this foot? Why is it so important." He picked it up and turned it over in his hands, looking at the huge hole in the bottom of the foot.

"Nate," Zeta said, "your face."

Nate looked up. "What?" he said, before looking over at Edgar and Phaedra, "what's wrong with my face."

"Didn't... didn't you have a scar?" Edgar said. Nate quickly ran his fingers up to his temple, down the side of his face where his childhood scar had always been. It was gone. The flesh was smooth and soft, unmarred in any way.

"My scar!" he yelled, bolting into the bathroom and flicking on the light. He looked at himself in the mirror. It was like looking at a different person. He knew what he looked like, sure, light brown hair and pointed chin, but his eyes always were drawn to the scar on his face, the one feature blurring out the rest. Suddenly, the reflection he'd looked at his whole life was different, the scar was completely gone.

He wandered back into the dining room, where the others stared at him. "The scar is gone. The foot... the foot healed my face."

"Holy shit!" Edgar yelled, cigarette dropping from his mouth in awe, "your face... my face! I can get my fucking face back! Fuck you, Tarentola! I'm getting my face back!"

Edgar snatched the foot up from the table and held it to his bare chest. Everyone stood in silence, and nothing happened.

Then, slowly, the cuts on his chest started shrinking, skin pulling together, meshing itself. The scratches on his arms faded, cuts on his hands sealing closed, leaving not even a red mark where they had been. Edgar looked around wildly, entire body tingling, slightly numb, but he felt the first tendrils of flesh extending from the ragged edges of his hairline across his forehead, up his jaw and in from his cheekbones. He could see them connecting under his eyes, building a bridge under the mushrooming cartilage of his nose, forming his lips. He felt the hair sprouting from his eyebrows, a beard starting on his fleshy chin. He felt cheeks spanning from cheekbone to jaw, nostrils sculpting themselves, eyelids forming over his dry and sore eyes. He extended his tongue to lick his lips, blinked to verify that his eyelids were whole, that his face had returned.

"Did it work?" he said, his voice soft and smooth, looking around at his dumbfounded friends. They stared at him, stared at the newly formed flesh and hair.

"Edgar," Nate said, "you... uh... didn't happen to look a whole lot like Jesus, did you?"

"Jesus!?!"

Now Edgar ran off to the bathroom, staring at himself in the mirror. Jesus Christ looked back at him. Soft eyes, long beard, delicate features, none of it was reminiscent of Edgar's previous face. He ran from the bathroom. "Jesus!" he yelled. "I'm Jesus! What the fuck is going on? I'm Jesus!"

Then Nate got it. The mystical healing foot. The angels. The hole going through the foot. He grabbed the foot and ran to the door.

"Nate! What the fuck are you doing?" Edgar yelled.

Nate stopped at the door. He turned, pale and sweating. "This is the foot of Jesus Christ," he gasped.

Everyone stopped short, looked on wide-eyed, quietly trying to comprehend what they were seeing.

"Well," Edgar said, breaking the silence, "so much for Easter."

Nate turned swiftly and yanked open the door, racing from the house. Phaedra followed closely behind him. "Hey! What are you doing?"

"I don't know! I can't have the foot of Jesus Christ! I can't! We have to take it back! We have to put it back in the oil and pretend that we never saw it!"

"Yeah," Phaedra said, following Nate out the front door of the house into the cool darkness of the desert, "yeah! That's what we can do! No one saw us, right? There's no one out there! We can take it back, put it in the oil..."

"I spilt out the oil!"

"We can buy oil! We can stop and buy oil! We can do this!"

Nate jumped into the driver's side of the pickup truck and slammed the rusty door shut. He realized there still was no key for the truck, just exposed wires, and although he'd seen Edgar spark the truck into life a half-dozen times, he'd never actually done it himself. "Hold it! I'll start this thing!" Nate handed the leathery black severed foot out for Phaedra, who stood on the passenger's side, to take.

"I don't want it!" Phaedra yelled back into the cool night air, hands up.

The driver's side window exploded in a shower of shattered glass. Nate shook his head, clearing the chunks of glass from his hair. He ducked down in his seat, while Phaedra, her military training telling her that a vehicle was not adequate cover, leapt towards the house, rolling midway and swerving as she ran to avoid possible gunfire. She ducked into the house and slammed the door shut.

Nate looked out. It was Michael Jackson, black hair thick and partially covering the cross stamped into his delicate waxy forehead. Behind him, though, in the darkness, were shadows, silhouettes of dozens of things, some human looking, some not, hot steam rising from their bodies into the cool air, lit only by the floodlight of Nate's house.

"The foot of Jesus of Nazareth," the Pope said, emerging from the bodies of the dozens of darkened forms, "give it to me!"

35

Nate got out of the truck, a waterfall of glass shards spilling out from the interior, and held the foot in his hands. "Pope, all due respect, but no fucking way," he said defiantly, yet a slight waver in his voice revealing his uncertainty.

That was all it took. The Pope lunged forward, lithe for a man of his years, wielding the razor-sharp crosier and slashed Nate across the belly, spilling his entrails out onto the hard packed earth.

Nate doubled over, curling his body over to protect his intestines and viscera. Edgar appeared from behind the back of the truck.

"Avert your eyes," he said, raising his arms ceremoniously. He had a bed sheet wrapped around his shoulders and was trying to make his Jesus face look as authentic as he could. The creatures halted, frozen in place from reverence. "You unworthy... pheasants... take not of my foot... uh..."

"False prophet! Blasphemer! Desecrator!" the Pope yelled, the creatures of darkness behind him howling in fury.

"Uh, give Jesus a second here," he said, holding a finger up. He leaned over Nate, whose intestines had miraculously retracted into his body, the gaping wound stitching itself together by the power of the holy foot. "Nate, I have to tell you something."

"What," Nate said, excruciating pain still shooting through his entire abdomen. Even though the laceration was being healed rapidly, the pain still bit into him, unbearably.

"We're... uh... way out of our depths here. Only one thing to do," he said, and turned. "Run for it!" he yelled, swiftly sprinting from the horde.

"Now, the foot," the Pope said, turning his attention away from the false Jesus and back onto where Nate should have been, but in front of him, between he and the brown pickup truck was just a puddle of blood on the ground. Nate skittered around the corner of the house and out into the open desert, running madly, all out, foot clutched tightly to his chest.

"This isn't good," Phaedra shouted to Zeta, looking out of the front door where she'd retreated. Her instinct was to protect the civilians. Zeta was closest, and seemed the most vulnerable. She shut the door, locking it. "We need to find some cover. This place got a cellar?"

There wasn't a moment before the door burst inwards. Standing on the other side was a woman, a Stigmatic, blood tears streaming down her face from her stitched up eyes, clad in what looked like the Shroud of Turin, with blood dripping from her hands, sanguine puddle around her bare feet.

"Stay back," Phaedra said, backing away, wishing she had her rifle. She picked up a chair to hold in front of her like a lion tamer. Subtly at first, a green glow tinged the room, then brighter as Phaedra grew more and more alarmed, more afraid for her own life, until her irradiated skeleton shone brightly through her skin. "You don't want to be on the wrong side of a piledriver, bitch!"

Outside, Nate groped his way through the desert, falling and then scrambling to get back to his feet. He could hear hoof beats behind him, approaching faster. He couldn't outrun horses, but, turning, he realized that these were not horses chasing him. Even by the dwindling evening sunlight, he could see they had human faces! They were horses with angry human faces, long hair, and armoured with golden helmets and barding. They gnashed their terrible teeth, whipped their long, thin scorpion tails, as they swiftly closed the distance between themselves and Nate. Nate backed away, then one of the horrible creatures called Abbadon's Locusts slammed into him, knocking him to the ground, hooves bashing his body terribly as it passed over him.

Then the beating of wings, the wind, and a thump as the Sedia Gestatoria hit the ground, single-winged cherubs absorbing part of the impact with their slender legs.

Nate felt for the blackened foot. It wasn't in his hand any longer. He quickly looked around, but in the encroaching darkness, he couldn't find it. Abbadon's Locust, the huge horse with the demonic human visage, leaned in close, teeth gnashing closer and closer to his own face.

Snap!

The head of the creature was wrenched to the side, and then it fell, collapsing in stages, first the knees, then rolling onto its side. Eventually, mercifully, the head stopped lolling around on its broken neck and rested on the ground. Behind the massive creature, another creature, more massive, hairy and stinking, stood, teeth bared, muscles tense. Nate, for a moment, recognized the smell from the abandoned military camp, and looking up at the Bigfoot, feared for his life again.

"You got him, honey!" a man yelled. Nate looked around swiftly, seeing the outline of a small, wiry man, cheering the Bigfoot on.

The Pope, deadly hooked crosier extended once again, advanced upon the Bigfoot. Then, emerging from a small grove of mesquite trees, six more Bigfoot rose, towering, and the Pope slowly backed up.

Zeta walked calmly from the house. She wandered out through the laundry room door, off of the back porch, and out into the dark desert. Inside Phaedra backed up, too, but slowly, giving no opportunity for the bloody-handed woman to attack. The Stigmatic walked forward in a fugue-like state, head askew and eyes crying tears of blood.

"Aren't you tired?" the Stigmatic asked, her voice much softer than Phaedra would've expected.

"No..." Phaedra said, after a moment of contemplation. It was a strange, sensitive moment. This woman, more monstrous than human, asking a rather pleasant question.

"You're tired, aren't you?" the Stigmatic asked again, her voice sweet, like warm wax pouring in Phaedra's ear. Then it hit her. Her eyes were, indeed, getting heavy, and she had to stifle a yawn. This woman was doing something to Phaedra, mesmerizing her with her voice, and it was working. Phaedra stumbled backwards, vision growing darker at the corners.

"It's all right," the stitch-faced woman said, wiping her bloodied hands on her robe, "you've done enough. Dream, my sister, dream."

"Yeah..." Phaedra mumbled, then, drawing up all her strength into her arms, she lifted the chair over her head. "Dream..." In her clouded mind, the crowd started cheering, slowly, quietly at first, but then the applause, the whistling and hooting, grew increasingly boisterous. Her military garb was gone, transformed into a black singlet, glowing bones stitched to the stretch fabric. Osama Akbar on his knees in front of her. "Oh yeah, I have plenty of dreams!"

With one swift movement, she slammed the chair down on the Stigmatic's head, dropping the bloody woman to the floor. Phaedra stared at her, backdrop of the wrestling ring and cheering crowd fading away, and the busted remains of the chair in her hand. Quickly, she turned and ran out the back door.

Nate peered around in the darkness, trying to make out shapes. He couldn't tell where who was friendly and who wasn't, who was a monster and who was... well, everyone he knew seemed like a monster now. Then, suddenly, he became acutely aware that people were running towards him. Giant men, lion faced, naked Men of Moab, clawed hands vicious and keen edged. The first was tackled by a Bigfoot, massive and thick, and the two creatures tumbled off into the darkness. Another Bigfoot was snatched up around the throat by the long, extended limb of a melted-faced Adolph Hitler. "Ich werde dich töten!" Hitler yelled, his voice gurgled, stiff wax wedges cracking on his drooping face. The Bigfoot struggled, clawing handfuls of wax out of the enlongated arm, but Hitler maintained his grip. Then, Hitler sneered, grip tightened and a horrible crunching sound came from the Bigfoot. Its arms went limp, and Hitler dropped the beast to the ground.

"My brother!" Umba yelled in horror. "What have I done?"

Phaedra leapt through the air, slamming Michael Jackson to the ground with a body slam that rivalled that of the Buckshot Kid. Jumping on the King of Pop she pinned him to the ground and slammed her glowing fists down into his face. Michael Jackson's face, distorted by each concussive fist worse than any plastic surgery, finally melted into a pile of waxy goo as Phaedra managed to distort the stamped cross beyond recognition. Michael Jackson was dead. Again. "Nate!" she yelled out, "we're getting killed out here!"

Nate looked over at the glowing skeleton in the darkness. Now, nothing phased him.

Umba knelt over the body of the fallen warrior, the Bigfoot that had given its life because of his own bizarre quest, his irrational journey into the desert. He wept for his brother, sobbing deeply, tears seeping into the stringy fur of the dead creature.

"You came," Zeta said, looking at the man. "She said you would."

He looked up at her. The face seemed familiar. The voice was the one that spoke to him deep down into his soul. Then he saw the semi-clad feral women, Tartarak Cannibal Girls, breaking towards them from the chaos around them. Tartarak Cannibal Girls were advancing upon them, the vicious women in tattered rags, filthy, scarred across their faces and hands, cheeks cut back to the jawline to allow them huge gaping mouths with horrifically sharpened teeth.

Nate was surrounded by chaos. The Pope had backed off into the darkness of the night, but danger was everywhere. One of Abbadon's Locusts raced by, straddled by a Bigfoot that was beating on the back of its head while it stung the Bigfoot across the back with its long scorpion tails. A single-winged cherub swept down from the blackened sky, tackled the glowing skeleton, a strobe light effect as they tumbled to a halt. The strange old man was ducking under the huge arms of a light brown bigfoot, keeping Zeta safe as it beat a half dozen naked women with its huge hammer-like fists.

But off in the distance, Brooke stood still.

Her clothes were ragged, her hair fallen out, but strong. Stronger than she'd been in decades. She stood, triumphant, surrounded by her new family, the huge, dog-like beasts who had nursed her back from dehydration and starvation with the demonic mother's milk of a lactating female. They had made her one of their own, socially and physically. Even the spikes were starting to emerge from her spine from the transformative properties of the creamy secretion. She stood and watched the pitched battle, violent screams of pain and anger echoing into the night.

"Fuck it," she said, and loped off into the night with the rest of the Chupacabra.

And the battle continued, Nate, feeling horribly outnumbered as he withstood the onslaught of the Pope's minions, crawled on his hands and knees. If he had the foot, he might be able to save himself, save some of his friends.

Nate looked up and realized that he was looking into the distorted visage of Adolf Hitler. Adolf's face twisted into an approximation of a sneer across his warped face.

"Don't... don't hurt me..." Nate managed to sputter out.

Blam! Blam! Blam!

Hitler turned, two more bullets seared through his flesh, one striking the middle of his forehead directly.

Blam! Blam!

Hitler fell to the ground. Nate looked around,and from the darkness it looked like Jesus was shooting a rifle. It wasn't Jesus. It was Edgar, Phaedra's M16 rifle in hand. He sidled up to him. "You didn't actually think I'd leave this in the desert," he said, over the racket of the ongoing battle.

He looked over and saw a naked cannibal girl get tackled by a rat kid, the unmistakable screeching sounds emanating from the beast, its claws digging into the cannibal's exposed flesh. He looked over at Edgar, who shrugged and continued firing into the desert night. "Do unto others," Edgar yelled into the blackness, firing dozens of rounds off at unseen targets, "before they do unto you!"

The war was turning. Another Bigfoot fell on the battlefield. Their numbers just weren't adequate, even with their mightiest warriors their opponents just kept coming and coming, seemingly endlessly. The Sisters of Eternal Torment arriving, blood red nuns' robes, cowls that covered their entire faces save for two black pinholes for them to see, flagellatory whips and misericords stabbing and hacking at the Bigfoot. Phaedra was swarmed by three, then four cherubs, each one biting at her flesh, ripping at her.

Zeta looked upon all of the carnage, all the bloodshed and gore, and reeled back in horror. She'd heard that Earth was a violent place. She'd learned about the wars, the atrocities, but it seemed academic at the time, stories her mother told her to remember her heritage, but seeing the blood, the death and cruelty, it was all too much. Then, from across the battlefield, a single three-sided blade, a misericord, knocked from the grip of one of the sisters came soaring towards her. With a sickening thunk, it buried itself into her shoulder, painfully, deep purple blood spraying across her face and body.

She didn't scream. She didn't flinch or cry out at all. Instead, she looked to the sky, concentrated for a moment, and then a low hum started reverberating across the landscape. It grew louder and louder. Suddenly, the entire desert floor was bathed in an unearthly white light, blinding, radiant. Everything was exposed, the menagerie of creatures, the waning numbers of Bigfoot, the old wildman of the woods, Jesus with a gun, and then, only paces away from Nate, the foot. Nate leapt at the foot, rolling across the ground as he snatched it up again into his grasp, and Edgar, weapon at the ready, covered him. Relieved to have retrieved the foot unnoticed by their enemies, Nate smiled up at Jesus, who gave him a discrete thumbs-up.

There was a sound, soft at first, then louder, like a digitized Tibetan bell, and six spheres of light coalesced, surrounded Zeta. The lights grew larger, more intense, and suddenly, beings materialized.

There were six of them, grey skin, bulbous heads with black bugged-out eyes, lipless mouths, wearing thin silver spacesuits. Each held what looked like a pistol, but yellow sparks flickered within the translucent cylinders, and there was what appeared to be a tiny satellite dish on the barrel of each one.

The beings started firing. Bursts of yellow light shot forth from their pistols in quick succession, flashing and illuminating the battle ground. One of the Sisters of Eternal Torment, charging the strange extraterrestrials with her bloodied misericord blade in hand, was hit, then exploded in a cloud of dust.

Fshhhow!

A beam of red light burst forth from above, hitting the ground with an explosive impact. Bodies flew in all directions, regardless of intent or aspiration. Only the small circle of silver clad beings was safe, and Zeta.

Fshhhow!

Again, and again, red desert dirt rained down upon them.

Then, nothing. The saucer-like ship above, red lights around its periphery showing it to be the size of a stadium, continued shining white light down, illuminating the ground below. Nate looked around, face aghast.

Death. Dead creatures, dead humans, dead Bigfoot, even the body of a rat kid sprawled out on the desert floor.

Phaedra crawled out from beneath a mass of cherub bodies. Her skeleton dim and she limped forwards towards Nate. Edgar put the barrel of the rifle on the firm desert floor, leaned on it, taking in the slaughter around him. Umba stood with Cinnamon.

Blood of dozens of beings seeped into the dirt.

They gathered together, not entirely aware of why Umba and the Bigfoot had helped them, not sure why the alien spacecraft had enacted such devastation. They had survived. They were alive, and that brought them together.

"Now…" the Pope said, emerging from beneath one of Abbadon's Locusts, ceremonial robes torn and bloodied, wielding his bladed crosier unsteadily, "for the last time, give me that foot."

Like a shot, the smallest rat kid, the last survivor of its kind, leapt from seemingly nowhere, clawing at the Pope, digging its yellow, splintered claws into the flesh of the old man. The crosier hit the floor, and Edgar was on it immediately.

"Fuck you, Vicar!" Edgar yelled, slicing the head cleanly off of the Pope.

The head fell to the ground, bloodlessly. The body fell to the ground with a thud, a flurry of activity beneath the skin of the pontiff. Writhing, wriggling beneath his holy robes.

Then, from out of the neck hole of the Pope, a weasel escaped into the desert night.

Then another, and another. Dozens upon dozens of weasels spurt forth from the severed neck of the Pope and skittered off into the darkness.

"The Pope was really just a big bag of weasels," Edgar said, looking up at the dumbfounded stares of everyone around him. "I knew it!"

36

"My mother sent you a message," Zeta said, the empty sack that was the Pope laid out flat on the desert floor at their feet, weasels all run off into the darkness. "She wasn't sure you'd get it. Your human physiology wasn't designed for psychic communications. You are Ambrose, yes?"

Nate sat with the foot on the ground in front of him, eyes glazed over with the enormity of the situation running through his wracked brain. He concentrated on breathing, occasionally putting his hand up to his face, a motion that once comforted him. He felt for that scar that had been with him for so many years, now gone, almost inexplicably so. Edgar was walking around, unfazed. He kicked at the fallen beasts, murmuring to himself as he looked at the strange amalgamations of creatures. Phaedra had her rifle back over her shoulder. She was simply trying to take in all that was around her.

"Ambrose," Umba muttered quietly, "it's been a lifetime since anyone has called me that. Yes, that was my name."

"My mother is Isabelle. She tells me that you once knew her," Zeta said, looking at the small, pitiable man. Zeta could see how scrawny he was, as compared to the other life forms she'd encountered here, how dirty and unkempt. She could see his eyes, soulful and confused, starting to leak little tears down his dirt-streaked face.

"You're Isabelle's daughter?" Ambrose gasped, "Oh my God! You've got her red hair! I don't know what to say! I've spent a lifetime wondering if she's all right! Where is she?"

"She's exceptional. She's had a remarkable life, for an Earthling. She found love. My father..." Zeta said, and then hesitated slightly, "...my father loved her. He died. He died. I believe it's been several years according to Earth's orbit."

"Oh god, I'm sorry..."

"She has been lonely. She talks about you, and about the life you could have shared. She said she once loved you, before she was taken away."

"She was abducted? So it's true? All these years and she was abducted by aliens?"

"It was a different time back then. You can imagine. Abductions are discouraged now, except for bovine life forms."

"I... I chased her off, though," Umba said, tears streaming down his dirty face, "I was young... impulsive..."

"That was long ago, and much has changed. You should see her now. Her skin has grown to a scintillating luminescence, her eyes, perfect glimmering jewels." Zeta looked up into the night sky, a smile emerging across her flawless pale features. "She is certainly the most beautiful woman in the galaxy." Zeta stepped closer to Umba, lifting his dark, worn hand in her own pale, impeccable one. "You must come with me, and spend the rest of your days being showered in her ephemeral beauty."

Decades of guilt, of suspicions and accusations, and most of all, loss, washed across Ambrose's mind. His life had been hard, spending most of it locked away in a cabin in the middle of nowhere, exposed to the elements day in and day out. So long he'd felt like the police would arrest him for the crime he never committed simply to close the case of Isabelle's disappearance. It was over, and maybe there'd never be any way he could prove it to anyone else, but he finally knew the truth.

Then he turned, looked over at Cinnamon. Her eyes wide and sad, as if she realized, ultimately, he wasn't truly Bigfoot. His type, the hairless pests who so often terrorized her kind with their machines, understood beauty in a different way than her own kind did.

"We must go. Our time here is at an end," Zeta spoke, her speech perfect English, no clicking or accent affecting her anymore. "My mother yearns for company."

"I don't mean to be contrary, but she cannot be the most beautiful woman in the galaxy," Umba said, his eyes not straying from Cinnamon's heavy brow, her thick features. "That distinction goes to my wife."

Cinnamon's eyes remained locked on Umba's, tears streaming down her dark, heavy face. Her lip quivered for just a moment. The understanding was clear.

"I told you, I only wanted closure. I have that. Isabelle has lived a good life, and so have you and I. She's always just been a memory, and maybe a memory of what I thought my life would be like. I have you, and that's all I ever wanted."

She knelt before him, so they could be face to face. He smiled, and then kissed her, deeply, passionately.

"Let's go home."

"Okay," Phaedra said, looking over at the long bearded face of Edgar, "that was a little weird."

"From what I know on my own world," Zeta said, smiling as Umba and Cinnamon walked off into the desert, arm in arm, "love is always a little weird."

"Well, I guess this Pope is done with," Edgar said, kicking the Pope sack on the ground, "but the Military isn't going to be done with us so quickly. This foot is way too hot a property to have around."

"I will take it," Zeta said pragmatically. "We are returning home. I will leave it on a deserted planet. You will never be burdened with it again."

"Oh," Nate said, rising to his feet. He brushed himself off, realizing how futile it was considering how much blood had soaked into his ripped and dirty sports shirt, "I was hoping that, you know, you'd stay for a bit." He looked at her perfect features, eyebrows raised.

"Is this an attempt at romance?" Zeta asked, matter-of-factly. She smiled a strange confused smile. "I'm not accustomed to your ways, so please forgive my confusion. I have a life elsewhere, and I'm returning to it. Without you. I'm sorry if you were hoping for any other outcome. I'm only half human, and to be honest, I identify more with my father's side."

Then, darkness. The bright light of the alien spacecraft no longer illuminating the desert floor and scattered carnage, and moments later, another light, a single beam, directly on Zeta and her six bodyguards. Lifting from the ground, she simply raised her hand in a final farewell.

37

Two weeks later, Nate stood at the Red Valley Cemetery. His father was dead.

It had nothing to do with the Pope, creatures in the darkness, faceless men or aliens. He had a stroke. Nothing more. A mere blood clot in his brain. A mundane death.

And Nate cried. The priest spoke in religious phrases that no longer had any meaning to him.

Werner's tired old friends gathered around, some wearing uniforms, some without. Merle and Arland looked on sombrely. Mr. Leone, Hardy, Dasha, and Mike Rant came to support their newest star journalist, and Nate cried. He leaned on Edgar, who, with a shave and a haircut, looked less and less like Jesus, although still had the soft features, the soulful eyes. To Edgar, it was better than no face at all.

Phaedra wasn't there. She had left, returned to the military, shamefully turning herself in for abandoning her post, even though she was unconscious at the time. She sat in the military prison outside of Pronghorn Mesa, awaiting her trial, unaware of the funeral, unaware of anything that happened after that night in the desert. She accepted her fate, or so she thought.

They'd pressed her for details. That was regulation, but somehow Phaedra realized she couldn't tell them everything. She could tell them about hallucinations, about the civilians who rendered aid to her. The Pope? Aliens? Bigfoot? She couldn't talk about that. They'd never believe her anyway, but certainly it was restricted information, much above the rank of an MP. They knew she'd abandoned her post. That's all. She couldn't even tell them about the foot. It would probably be better to leave out the part where she broke into the shack.

"Soldier," Colonel Nine barked, "it's good to see you. They treating you well here?" A guard walked up to him, but with a quick nod, the guard realized that Colonel Nine was a superior, and walked away.

"Colonel Nine!" Phaedra said, jumping to her feet and standing at attention. "I am sorry, sir. I failed to guard the post."

"Yeah," Colonel Nine said, hoisting up his pants, "I know. Couldn't resist going in that shack, could you? How long did you last?"

"Uh... about a couple of weeks... I think?" She furrowed her brow, realizing that she hadn't told anyone about breaking into the shack, but somehow he knew about it.

"Good. Walk with me, soldier," he said, turning on his heel and walking away from her cell. Phaedra protested for a moment, but he'd already walked away, so she quickly followed after him.

"I can't leave my cell," she said.

"There'll be no trial," Colonel Nine said, winking at her, "we take care of our own. So, I take it the foot is gone?"

"Yes sir, the foot is gone. I did my best, but I was... psychologically compromised at the time."

"Ah, well, that's the way the cookie crumbles," Colonel Nine laughed. "As long as the Pope doesn't have it, that's all I care. You did good, soldier."

Phaedra stiffened, eyes wide. "You... you know about the Pope? You know... everything?"

"Everything. Pretty much played out exactly as I thought it would. Except the Bigfoot. Who'd have thought they'd get involved, am I right?" Colonel Nine laughed a deep belly laugh as they walked out the front doors of the military prison, completely unimpeded. "My COs are impressed. General Four especially likes your tenacity. Now, let me talk to you about your next assignment."

And back in Red Valley, they lowered the casket into the ground. They turned and walked away. There'd be no wake, not even coffee and egg salad sandwiches. It was just another old man dying in another small town. Merle and Arland, away from their storytelling session at the Lucky, shook Nate's hand and invited him to sit with them anytime.

"It's tough," Edgar said, once out of earshot of the rest, "losing a father. I lost mine young. Never really processed it. Just kind of became a thing."

"It feels like I lost mine young, too," Nate said, "he was never a father. He was just some guy, some asshole who made my life miserable. I think I'm mourning the father that I wanted. The one who listened to me, taught me how to do things. Maybe bought me a birthday present now and then. That's who I'm mourning. Werner was just a sad man, had no way to express himself other than anger, and then lost his mind. That's all. It's just sad."

They walked over to the other new grave in town. Beatrice Hetherington. She was found in her house earlier in the week, alone, like she'd spent her life. It wasn't common to have two funerals in a week. Not in Red Valley. With Stan's house suddenly abandoned, and now that Beatrice was gone, their neighbourhood was looking pretty sparse. They'd find someone to take over at the library, probably one of the kids just out of high school, and they'd sell off her house, donate the money to the library in her name. Beatrice's body was found with a scratch on her face, but otherwise, it was simply assumed that she died of old age. Her heart stopped. Little did anyone know that somewhere beyond, not Heaven nor Hell, not a dream but not reality, Beatrice lived on, sleeping her nights away in the lush forests and dancing her days away with her strange, rat-like lover.

Nate and Edgar drove home in the pickup truck. Nate had gotten it fixed up, re-keyed so that he could drive it. The neighbourhood mechanic tuned up the engine, replaced the oil and put on a new set of tires. That old truck was a workhorse, and although ugly, it was exactly the type of vehicle Nate needed out in the desert. He pulled up to the house, pale blue boards still splintered at the edge where Elvis had attacked it.

"So what are you going to do now?" Edgar asked, slamming the passenger's side door. "Selling the house? Going back to your fancy city life?"

"No, I kind of like working at the Real World Monitor. The staff are insane, and I mean each and every one of them is insane, but they're decent people, and I kind of like knowing what's really going on in the world."

"I knew it!" Edgar yelled, "I knew you'd come around!"

They walked into the house, and the creak of the door was followed quickly by the scampering of clawed feet across the faded linoleum. The last remaining rat kid came racing up to them. It circled around Nate, rubbing his face on Nate's legs. Nate leaned down and rubbed the poor little rat-kid's furry chest. "I'm home, Werner" Nate said.

And far off across the desert, a young Chupacabra, smallest of its pack, spines still emerging from its canine backbone, followed along behind its elders, and the strange human that they had taken in. It stopped, sniffed the ground, and found a small morsel of flesh, dried out from the desert sun. It chewed the leathery flap of skin, swallowed roughly, then sniffed around more. It found a briefcase, and the butchered body of the man in the white lab coat, the one they had feasted upon only weeks ago. There was a short, curt yelp from the human, and the young Chupacabra loped off after her, into the boundless desert.

38

It was a chilly morning in Washington, DC. Melissa Virgo didn't know it, though. She'd been working throughout the night. Everyone on their floor had. The satellites had been going crazy.

It had all started with a blip earlier in the week. Something had appeared, momentarily, in the upper atmosphere. It must've been a glitch, everyone thought at first, as the thing must have been bigger than a cruise ship, and floating above the desert. It was crazy, and then, when it blipped out of existence, a full diagnostic cycle had been run on every computer in the building.

"Flock of birds," Mr. Palomar, her supervisor, had said. That made no sense. A flock of birds wouldn't appear in the middle of the night, with that massive density, and then disperse that quickly. Mr. Palomar was a bit of an ass, in Melissa's opinion.

The diagnostics had proven absolutely nothing. No problems, everything running well. Nothing even needed an update. So, life had continued on, documented but then ignored.

Until it happened again.

The previous night it appeared again. This time, it stayed. It stayed for ten minutes, hovered close to a small town in the middle of the desert. Red Valley. By the time they got the word out to the police, though, it was over. Eyewitness reports had been scattered. Some saw a huge saucer out above the desert, others saw a small booth being held aloft by angels. One person claimed to have seen Michael Jackson.

This was the problem with investigating unexplained phenomenon. Once someone asks the question about something extraterrestrial, people start making stuff up in order to get on the news. It was all too unreliable, too unscientific, and Melissa Virgo was only interested in what could be observed and proven. What she did know, though, was that the blip on the satellites, the massive object floating above the desert, that had shown up on radar. That was something, and until proven to be some sort of computer malfunction, she had to take it seriously.

But while Mr. Palomar eventually took the blip seriously, it was obvious he didn't take her seriously. She got bumped off of the satellite. She had to cover for the astrophysicist who was working on the Mars Atmosphere and Volatile Evolution Mission satellite, known as the MAVEN. She was pulling a double, as was most everyone in the building. Everyone was busy trying to figure out what the blip was. Everyone was examining the information, hoping for evidence of extraterrestrial life, and while monitoring the data from MAVEN was important, it wasn't the blip. It wasn't where the action was.

That's when it happened.

It appeared on her long range scanners. Roughly the same size and shape as the blip over the desert.

"Hey! I got something!" she yelled out, and the rest of the scientists in the dark room looked up, "It's approaching Mars!"

There was a flurry of activity surrounding Melissa's workstation. A dozen scientists hustled in close, edging each other out for a better position to see what was happening on her screen. Mr. Palomar waddled his huge posterior over from his workstation, too.

"Look at the size of it," one of the scientists mumbled behind her. She switched from screen to screen. She'd sent a message to the MAVEN to track it, but with the time it took to change camera angles, it'd be minutes before it even got the message.

Then they saw it. Sparkling, a gleaming silver behemoth rimmed by lights in the darkness of space. From their distance, they could calculate the image size against the radar imagery. It was huge. It was larger than any man-made object in space. As it approached the satellite, closer and closer, it showed very little detail. It filled camera four fully, but no seams in the metal structure were visible. There was no writing, no edges, just a huge, reflective, unblemished surface.

Then a seam appeared. A square hole, a port of some sort spilling light out into the darkness of space.

"What the Hell is that?" Melissa said to no one in particular, engulfed in her screens. Still, a half dozen people behind her mumbled. Had they taken a moment to return to their own workstations they could've pulled up the stream on their own computers, but none of them wanted to miss a single second of this history making event.

"Ok," Mr. Palomar announced, "move off this station. Let me take over."

"It dropped something!" she said, Mr. Palomar's words not even making an impression. She couldn't be sure of what it was, but she saw it. Maybe it was just a pixel of shifting light, but she saw it, something small escaping the portal, and it had moved, quickly, before disappearing off of the screen.

Then the ship darted off camera. She shifted her view to camera seven, then ten, and caught a glimpse of it as it disappeared into the void of space, faster than physics should allow.

Everyone stood there, astonished. It was all recorded, all documented. They'd be going over this footage for the next ten years, gleaning every iota of information that they could. There were laughs of disbelief behind Melissa as everyone tried to wrap their brains around the fact that for the first time in recorded history they may have just seen evidence of extraterrestrial life. Aliens. Even Mr. Palomar was stunned into silence, which had never happened as long as anyone had known him.

But Melissa didn't laugh in disbelief. She swapped through camera after camera, sending signals to zoom, knowing it may be too late.

She followed the trajectory, and, with luck beyond luck, saw a tiny speck of light as the dropped object passed through the thin atmosphere of Mars.

"I've got it!" she yelled, and suddenly every eye was back on her screen. "The thing they dropped! It's heading for the Cydonia region!" They knew the Cydonia region because it was a huge dark-coloured plain, but the object was heading towards the north end of Cydonia, a rocky region known as the Cydonia Colles.

"Where's it going?" a scientist yelled, but Melissa was already working on it. She worked out the trajectory swiftly in her head.

"40.75° north latitude and 9.46° west longitude," she said, then wondered a moment why this seemed familiar to her.

"The face…" Mr. Palomar whispered over her shoulder, leaning in close to look at the screen, "it's heading for the face on Mars."

Before they could comprehend his statement, she knew that it had impacted. Given the trajectory and the velocity, she knew it must have it.

"The face on Mars. What a coincidence," she said, smiling at the odds, "that'll surely give the conspiracy nuts something to…"

But her words were cut short. There was some sort of seismic activity on Mars. The ground where the cameras were pointed was shaking, red dust was engulfing the entire site, obscuring the face on Mars and all around it.

Then through the flurry of dust, what looked like a tremendous pillar thrust up through the clouds. Melissa squinted at her screen, trying to make out what it was despite the poor resolution. It was a hand! It was an arm!

Then, it stood up! A thousand feet tall for sure, red stone body, monumental and monstrous. It turned its face upwards to the dark sky, almost as if to look directly at the satellite itself, and although inaudible from space, it flexed its gargantuan muscles and let out a massive roar of rage and fury.

"Stop!" Mr. Palomar yelled. "Monitors off! No one... and this is under threat of termination... says anything to anyone... anyone at all, hear me... about what just happened!"

But Melissa, unknown to her supervisors and peers, was already mentally penning her letter to the Real World Monitor.

Brad Glenn is a writer, artist, and teacher in Edmonton, Alberta. He graduated from the University of Victoria from the department of writing, and has been writing fiction and poetry for the last  thirty years. In the last ten years Brad has been focusing his creativity creating comics and comic scripts, although has released a book of his short stories called Lemons on Venus.

In 1989 he was a security guard at a dangerous apartment complex, and amidst the anxiety of the job, and depression, he found a discarded garbage bag filled with issues of a certain tabloid newspaper. Those late stress-filled nights were accented by these stories of alien encounters and Michael Jackson sightings, and were the inspiration for this novel.

CPSIA information can be obtained
at www.ICGtesting.com
Printed in the USA
LVOW03s0318100917
547987LV00006B/7/P